READ/READ

(/ri:d/) *(/red/)*

Pia Bakshi

INKSTATE BOOKS

ISBN 978-93-52010-75-2

First published in India 2018 by Inkstate Books
An imprint of Leadstart Publishing Pvt Ltd

Sales Office:
Unit No.25, Building No.A/1,
Near Wadala RTO,
Wadala (East), Mumbai – 400037 India
Phone: +91 22 24046887

Editor: Shayoni Mitra
Cover: Pia Bakshi
Layouts: Ashwini Jadhav

To Dadaji,

for staying close.

Contents

About the Author

Pia's literary interests are found at the cusp of a world that is at once Kafkaesque and at once Romantic. A better part of her day goes in reconciling this binary.

An ardent student of literature, a scriptwriter and a language and elocution coach, she writes fiction inspired by Literary Theory particularly moved by Barthes and Rosenblatt and poetry inspired by collective and individual human experience. A Charles Wallace India Trust Fellow at SUISS, University of Edinburgh and a Young India Fellow with a Masters in Liberal Studies from Ashoka University, Pia practices Zentangle and Abstract Expressionism. She runs PhilARThropy, a volunteer driven social organisation, committed to creating an inclusive and accessible space for art through her work in under-resourced communities. She is a singer-songwriter who also plays the guitar and the ukulele.

Some of her songs also find mention in the book.

She can be reached at piabakshi@bluestockings.co.

Acknowledgements

I cannot offer enough gratitude to

-Ma and Pa for unabashed love, unrelenting support and for uninhibited conversations over walks that led to this story.

-My sister, Neha (she ensured that the manuscript was sent out while I chose to sit on it) and my Brother in Law, Siddharth, for being my firmest critics and most doting appreciators and for making me believe in the words I write.

-My friends (they know who they are) who made it easy to smile, laugh, cry, swoon and sing into oblivion along the process.

-Professor Saikat Majumdar for bringing out possibilities that I did not know I had in my writing.

-Tanya Mendonsa for her beautiful presence in my life through her words in print and our conversations.

-Aruni Kashyap for teaching me the art of talking to my characters.

-Professor Madhavi Menon for classroom epiphanies and redefining Frankenstein for me.

-Professor Nicholas Grene for giving me a definition of the abstract idea of home.

- My editor, Shayoni Mitra for her time and efforts in engaging with this project and her invaluable inputs.

-Bukowski for his words and crude honesty.

-Roland Barthes for The Death of The Author that first sparked this thought of investigating the creator and creation relationship in my mind.

-Ashoka University where I learnt what helped develop this story.

-The visceral marvel of Mumbai for always calling me back to visit its multitudes.

-Cliff Richard for Carrie, Lumineers for Ophelia, Dean Martin for Send Me The Pillow That You Dream On; Damien Rice for The Greatest Bastard; Tom Waits for Martha; Ben Zaidi for Ivory; Phosphorescence for Wolves; Taken by Trees for Only Yesterday; Saleem Raza for Ae Dil; Iron and Wine for Flightless Bird, American Mouth; Karen O for Moon Song, George Ezra for Budapest and Beatles for more than songs.

My place is the Placeless,
my trace is the Traceless;
'Tis neither body nor soul,

for I belong to the soul of the Beloved.

-Rumi

Read.
(/ri:d/)

I start on page one but I began before.

My voice was held in the tongues she touched with hers and the ones that touched her with their words. Like spring and cherry blossom. My body was born of the silhouette that followed her in the streets of Philly that she carries all the way to Malad East. My limbs stretched out like the driver of the Ola cab when his indicator refused to work and my legs stretched out of the running red bus as I jumped to stop at what was not the bus stand. My smell stays stained in Marlboro Lights' ash and Sula wine mixed with a wet bitch as she inches to her end. I smell Old Spice too, because she puts it on her wrist ever so often to smell him off her, again. My skin changed colour as I moved from Philly to Mumbai like the sun as it travels from the sky to the horizon. I am naked at the wrist where a watch tells me what the time is. It is a second hand watch from a nostalgia shop. It does not always tell the right time but it speaks of a time that belonged to someone I do not know. She likes that. Not knowing and she makes me wear it as a reminder of never knowing. I never know anything, anyway. I follow. She leads.

I dance my way to this completion. She says I swim. So,

I swim. Along the lapse I see faces - scarred, happy, smiling, burnt at the edges, stubble-d with a red lipstick on a hairless patch; hear old playlists -Roo Panes, Spice girls, Britney Spears and Damien Rice; smell the Philly sun drying the walls of her house and the walls that speak and Mumbai rain and how the sea changes its smell with it and watch all of them seep into my developing pores and reach an eggshell of my paper heart.

My lap ends.

I am born of others.

She wrote and I became. Every consonant wrapped around my neck like an umbilical cord and every syllable released it, one 'ah' after the other. With each vowel I stretched out my limbs, each word defined my toes and fingers. Each punctuation mark defined the sex I was going to belong to and I became a man because of the pauses and the exclamations, because of the question marks and the hyphens. A sentence ran like blood through my veins and somewhere a whole page gave me a cream white heart.

I was born of her language.

You touch the pages, often. Once you smelled me off the page too. I don't know my smell because I have nothing to compare it to but I like the idea of touch... It feels warm like the sun in Philly should have felt and that is enough for today.

Maybe tomorrow you will come back and read, too.

Maybe tomorrow you will
come back and read, too.

PART 1

EROS

To die, be born.
For the night, forget the dawn.

CHAPTER 1

I have a name, today.

I was created. I was made from scratch by a vowel intersecting a consonant.

Smith.

I am supposed to respond to this concoction of sounds. She tells me that I am from a street in Philly.

I only know lines on a page. Sometimes I live in the fifth line when someone says the word Smith.

Sometimes you will not find me till the end of the page. Is Philly like that?

If yes, then maybe I am from there.

Her mind tells me something her fingers do not. I can see her thoughts. I live in them, too - live as a permanent resident of the laptop screen but I go for an evening walk to her mind and her dreams.

Her mind sees stairs that lead up to a large building. She remembers herself jumping and throwing punches in the air when she climbs them. I wonder what that means but she looks happy and a little yellow is good for the colour I lack... She stands before an old house for long and just stares. Then she takes out a pen and a book to begin writing. She also runs her hands through the back walls of houses stacked together in the area she was forbidden to go to. She sees colours. She climbs on top of another building (I do not know the name because she does not think of names- She just thinks of the place and the feeling. I feel along) and looks at the skyline beyond the Delaware (she thinks of that name). She likes it. Water. She looks at it for hours. She looks at it and then at a neon banner on the roof of an opposite building that flickers. She hates flickering lights but she looks on. She sits on grass barefoot and reads.

She reads.

Me, she writes.

She wrote/typed down my name for the first time, today. For a very long time I was just the guy. I was the pronoun 'He'. Only today, someone at the end of the page called out to me and I was christened. So, no big ceremonies for me.

Just an accidental reference that I happened to respond to. She thought I should and so I did.

I am Smith. But I do not know if that is my first name or the last. She always signs off with Banks, her last name. But in her mind, she thinks of the letters 'EB' scribbled in different handwritings on crushed pages. Her name is Elixir. She sometimes makes it easier for me by fleshing out details in her mind. At least that is what I think.

So, Smith. I respond to this weird combination of a lisping *s* meeting a pursed *m* leading to an open *i* finding a *t* in the click of the tongue against one's teeth and then releasing the *h* through a little peephole made by the tongue with the mouth. You see a glimmer of white in the pink of the interiors. Maybe, you see the colour or the lack of it in my heart too through this word.

She talks to me sometimes. She talked to me more when she had not found a name for me. She questioned me and I tried to answer.

She said, "Hey, so what would you have done if you left your bag in GetAway Cafe?" I did not have the answer but I knew what running was. I ran across pages so that is what I said. She played along. I answered and she heard. Now, she has a name for me that I do not know. She asks me, "Smith, will you get your bag, today?" But today I do not have an answer. You see, I do not know who this Smith is.

Smith leaves his bag in restaurants. But I leave myself benched between sentences and pauses. Maybe, we are alike. This Smith and I.

Maybe.

She likes him. She spends a lot of time writing his story. She thinks it is my story too.

I will let her live with that. It makes her happy to think she knows me, that she creates me with every word that escapes the convoluted lines of her brain and rests on her tongue. She sometimes says them aloud and then, she types me down. Word by word. And I become.

But then she talks about this Smith and I am left as a pronoun in the beginning of a sentence and with a name at the end of it.

She reads what she writes and turns off the lamp. She closes the screen and I realise that my bed is the space between the screen and the keyboard. My bed is also her dreams. She does not realise that I do not sleep on the bed prepared for me but in her dreams where I escape to take a walk to know more about me, her and us - the ones that she chooses to continue in her mornings with her fingers and a keyboard.

I become of a dream.

Am I even real, then?

For now, I know I am someone called Smith, as long as he is the same 'He' I was and I am from Philly, as long as Philly looks like the A4 pages on a screen.

I belong here, in this sound and in this space, for now.

October 1, 2016
2:04 A.M.

Hey EB,

I could say more. I could write more. I want to. Because I know that is what you do - when you write songs, when you 'calligraph' others' words, when you fill a journal I do not get to read.

For now, let me tell you what I will miss when I move out.

I will miss the way I always woke with your Crimson Crunch, number 512, on my cheek on the part where a cigarette burnt my skin. You heal it with your kiss every morning.

It does not matter that you gave it to me. It will be like a tattoo you left on my skin. Permanent.

I will miss the honeycomb of your hair. Like a mesh I got lost in. I woke up with strands on my lips entering my mouth. I cribbed before. 'Why don't you tie your hair when you sleep?'

I think I will miss it now.

I will miss how you never finish what you start. How many folders do you have on your laptop?

Unfinished songs? Incomplete sketches in your journal? Dusting canvases - none painted?

I will miss Ginnie. I will miss her seeing me with her unseeing eyes. I will miss her. Yes. Maybe, the most. I will miss her fur under my feet when she lay under the mattress on the floor of the first apartment we moved into. I will miss waking up to her lick. I know I cringed but the wetness and its smell became familiar. So, I took her for all those walks in the morning where she peed against the lamppost where I was singing when you met me and dropped a coin into my open guitar case. All I saw was your disappearing silhouette. I kept singing hoping you would look back.- I remember I was singing Cliff's Carrie that night- but you did not look back even then.

Look back now, maybe?

I will miss how we finished Fleishmann's Preferred every week and the Glenfiddich we drank every time I got a gig that no one came for and you published on that silly blog of your silly friend. And how we cribbed when the fridge had nothing to offer on hungover mornings.

I will miss how you shouted at me for not fixing the faucet.

I will miss walking with you quietly. Not saying a word. Not filling silences.

I will miss you humming Avril Lavigne and laughing when I caught you. How could you?

I will miss silently judging you.

I will miss you shouting at me on 7th Street looking at a whitish door where one of your fancy poets lived and wrote (I cannot remember his name because I never liked him). How many times, EB, will you live through others?

I will miss you throwing water on me when I refused to wake up in time for my gig at GetAway Café.

It is hard to wake up at 2 A.M. But you were always awake at night. You and Ginnie.

You looked at me as if I was doing something stupid by sleeping.

I will miss that look.

I will miss how you looked in that black torn bra and my polka dotted boxers.

-the bra that is torn where it sits between your breasts. It made foreplay easy.

I will miss your morning breath. You kissed that cigarette gash before brushing and I could smell all the air you held in your mouth through the night. I preferred your Victoria Secret but this was mine and just mine to smell and taste.

I will miss the loose pages and lost pen caps spread all over the floor of our apartment.

I will miss the pained laptop cover you never used and the guitar you never played.

I will miss how you obsessed over what I sang because you hated it. You always tried writing for me and I never sang what you did. Guess what, EB? I sang your song when you chose not to come.

I sang that song when you chose to share your honeycomb and my Crimson Crunch with another man on our bed.

I sang that song, then.

I broke the painted guitar that you never played because I was angry. I am angry because you are moving away.

Because you cannot stand my stare anymore. You can't stand the guilt anymore.

I hate you for it. Go hide in front of the white door. You know I will not come looking for you, anyway. At least not there.

I hate you so much for it that I will not fix that bloody faucet. I will not and you will just have to deal with it.

Also, you cribbed how I never wrote anything from the heart. Well, I did.

It is for you.

It is a song for you because you have silenced mine.

I will miss you but I will miss my music more because every time I think of singing I think of you putting another man's junk in your mouth and I think of him kissing your skin made bare by the tear in my favourite black bra. I will miss my music. I will miss Ginnie. And I will miss seeing your face when you read the song.

I am going.

Before you get back, I will be gone.

I will miss you, EB. But I will miss what we had more.

You tore it apart, like the bra. And now you are moving away. Escaping, are you?

Escape, then. But I win here, too. I am escaping before you.

I am leaving with this song.

Play the tape in that music player you bought form the nostalgia shop/ old shanty in Mumbai even when I told you not to.

Go, play it, now.

I am gone but my voice will haunt you.

Also, get someone to fix that faucet. Or don't. You are moving away, anyway.

Fuck off, EB.

Just know I will miss you. Terribly. Soberly. Bitterly.

Yours, for now.

- T

⁂

The song: *for those who want to read (/ri:d/) it-*

I want my music back.
I want that melody to be mine again.
That riff, I composed that on a drunken night. No kid, not alcohol but thoughts. Did anyone ever tell you they are the most intoxicating?
That and expectations.
Oh boy, they make you delusional.

I want my music back.
That rhythm was the fast beating of my heart.
When you placed my hand on your waist like it was art.
When we danced till it was time to say goodbye.
No kid, not the physical goodbye. That happened years ago but this time my tears kissed you goodbye.
It wasn't the passionate French kiss we talked about on an actually drunken evening but a light peck on your puckered words.

I want my music back.
That interlude was me finding my way back to the chorus.
The chorus I sang in the shower thinking of you.
The chorus I sang for you when you came to hear my music, that night.
Did you know, I wrote that verse about you?
Later I sang the chorus in the shower with you.
How your eyes cast down every time you spoke;

How your mouth did that funny twirl before you joked;
How your words were your only freedom...
I set you free, my caged bird.

I want my music back.
And you don't even know you have it.
But I gave it away a while back.
Maybe one day, when you strum the f#, it will come to you.
And that day it will come back to me too.

⁕

I SANG THAT SONG, THEN.

#1
Dec 2, 2016
12:59 A.M

Tip.
Tip.
Tip.
Tip.

(Note to self - get that godforsaken faucet fixed)

Leaking faucets.

They have been a constant in my life - from Philly to Mumbai, from puberty to adulthood, from mistakes to corrections. They always drip and now, I treat their music as the unfailing soundtrack of my life.

I would have loved a Louis Armstrong but for now a faucet will have to do. I remember when even something as regular as a leaking faucet made me write the most ridiculous romantic poetry. It is strange that I still remember it. But, I was in love then, or so I thought.

It is easy to find a muse and then drain poetry through him. The pedestal this muse arrives at; the veneration it receives; the transition from *he* to it. How I dehumanised the only human I had in life... But look at Ginnie. Is she any less human? With her wise eyes milkying into blindness and her floppy ears hiding the gash she got from the corner of my side table when she ran around adjusting to darkness or that tail left wagging even in sleep. She dreams, just like me I guess... I think... I am almost sure... But I am always rambling... And digressing.

I wonder what my Professor would have said to me now if he realised I am writing a journal about how I am writing. We sat in a room with coffee coloured walls with maroon curtains browned at the end. But it smelled of books, that weird concoction of petrichor and Old Spice that I have associated (or liked to associate) with yellowing pages. You cannot kill a romantic completely now, can you? Maybe, you never can and never will. Maybe... Definitely. In specs, in eyes hidden behind cat eyed spectacles. *(I need to clean my specs - note to self)*

I write note to self as if someone is going to read this. This is all for self. Unless I die and become famous for my incoherent ramblings... The Rambler of Banal Thoughts, they'd call me. They love tags, don't they? Fit in one and bam! You are part of them. But I will be gone and for me it will always be for myself.

So, the Old Spice has stayed and the yellowing pages are still savoured. Somewhere in this Old Spice, I smell Ginnie - that wet dog odour *(she fell into a puddle again - get a leash: another note to self)*

that smells like home, now.

And, I digress again. He warned me against it. He said in his voice as red as the curtains covering his windows, "Organise your thoughts. Reading your paper felt like finishing a 10 km run on the treadmill. I had to run to keep up."

He said something about how it felt victorious to finish it and he liked the challenge but everyone won't. And he was right. No one has, till now.

My father and I went to this Xerox shop back in Philly. He could never understand machines and my limited knowledge was a marvel to him. So, I went with him. This little room under a shop sold electronics at cheap rates - at least that is what the board said. What I loved was the wall beneath K's Hardware Store, holding the white door to the Xerox shop. That was a long time ago when walls spoke to me and I talked back. Pa and I talked to them together sometimes. He never found it weird. He let me indulge in it. How can you not talk to colours?

But mostly, how can you not talk to dirt smeared over the colours? Their stories are brilliant. At least the ones I made, I realise now. How did they reach the wall? Did a car drive by? Pa nodded with a maybe. My favourite nod... Because it was not a definitive answer, Just possibilities. Like the dirt on the walls... Or the one on my specs... Like the one on the screen of my laptop...

So, the Xerox shop.

Tak.
Tak.
Tak.
Tak.

The churning of the printing machine and the words we spoke in between. He made me print this piece that told me that *I was complete in my own being and that is what scared the world.* It had a picture of a father holding the end of the cycle as a little girl blissfully believed she was doing it on her own. Balance. Support. All that jazz in one simple picture. I look for that balance, but it is hard to find and I don't really have someone tugging at the end of this cycle. But there is Ginnie tucked in a pile of my clothes at my feet. I remember tearing up a little and back then, the sultry summer sweat helped in hiding the streaks benched at the edge of my upper lips.

So *tak tak tak* reminds me of just that moment. Maybe that is why I type when I work on my manuscript. I feel complete with the *tak tak tak*. I feel connected. *Tip tip tip* on the other hand confuses me.

It is not summer heat sweat. It is water falling from the AC's vent when I am having a good dream.

It is not like the one-size-fits-all bra I found on Linking Road. It is like a trial room with beautifully photoshopped models with the biggest junk and somewhere between them my reflection.

I am proportionate and maybe even pretty by magazine standards but the reflection is sandwiched between perfection and that isn't palatable.

It is not the *pitter patter* of rain that Ginnie raises her ears and white eyes for, but that leaking faucet that does not stop and that face -

The face with its ridges and its stubble growing incongruously - too much on the left cheek and a little on the right; a cigarette stub that scarred him of barrenness on that cheek for the rest of his life. That was my favourite part. I always left a kiss there. The Crimson Crunch of my 4.99 bucks lipstick stayed there in its chapped glory. It was that ridge that was important.

Because he washed it ducked under the same tap. This is where we stayed for a week when we first visited. Now, I have come back here but alone.

That godforsaken tap does not stop leaking and I wake up and sleep to it.

My water tank gets drained every week but I don't have it in me to change the faucet. Why?

I don't know. I know for certain that my Professor doesn't have answers to this question. I know my father would but he is not around for tugging ends of my loose thoughts, now. Ginnie, do you know?

Earlier you could tell it was the tap and not rain. Now, you cannot. Does it matter?

You never liked going outside, anyway.

What was I writing about, again?

I have smeared ash on the pages before me again. And stubbed the pages, again. Even the page burns before me but the tap leaks. Without purpose.

Tip.
Tip.
Tip.

I remember what I started writing about. I remember that soppy little piece by heart.

What are Monday nights for you?
Are they muffled in the discomfort you feel in your tail bone every time you squirm because of that fall because of that reckless stunt in bed? I told you your back couldn't take it, even then.
That is all that I was, wasn't I?
-A reckless stunt;
a thoughtless mistake;
or is it knitted in the familiarity of old pyjamas with torn pockets, the one you wore on that Monday night, a year ago, when you stayed over.
Does your back still hurt?
Does someone make your back hurt?
Is someone else, the new reckless stunt?

For me, these Monday nights are full of memories-where I sit with a laptop in front of me and words streaming down the tips of my fingers like water from a tap.
Drip by drip.
No matter how hard I turn the knob and try to stop the flow, it just flows.
I will call the plumber tomorrow.
and maybe he can fix the faucet.
I will call you tomorrow.
and maybe you can fix me.

It is strange that I don't miss the face and how it bruised my cheek anymore. I just cannot forget it. Maybe it is the tap. Maybe it is the fact that I cannot find Crimson Crunch in any store in Mumbai, not even in that Get-It-All shop at Colaba (just in case someone gets to read this and is also looking for that shade. It has gone forever. Accept it and move on) and I took that local from Goregaon to Churchgate to find the shade and nope, I found the one-size-fits-all bra in Bandra, a deep red in colour but not the red benched on a cigarette stubbed ridge on a cheek. I just want my red back.

That is why I save writing for the journal. It is dog eared, messy and confused like my mind.

I save my coherent words for the screen. The *tak tak tak* saves me from the *tip tip tip*.

For now, that will do.

It is raining today and the sound helps to ignore the leaking faucet. Ginnie agrees because she lies at my feet sleeping. I think she is dreaming too.

For the red, I find my Sula sitting on my bedside table. It is warm from being ignored last night. But I have my screen before me. And a story I glimpsed at in my dreams last night.

For now, that is enough.

⁕

CHAPTER 2

Today I am in a white shirt.

And a pair of blue jeans. Not quite blue. The colour of Delaware that she sees in her mind. It is a little murkier than the blue she sees of the Philly sky.

The sun seems to burn my skin and I am left with a tan the colour of milk tea- the kind made with love that always means a little more sugar and a little more milk.

She smiles as she writes this and I warm up to Smith more. He feels natural now.

Except for the white shirt and the blue jeans. My only adornments have always been the curves of black letters on the screen and almost always parts of me are left naked. You can only see Smith's arms and the base of his neck. She often thinks about someone's forearms. Hairy arms.

For me, you can sometimes see me through the gaping hole in 's' and the repeating curves of 'm'. Where do I lie? In the letters or somewhere benched between the lines in the nakedness through which the paper appears? The yellowing paper like tea with a lot of milk? Maybe, only milk and floating tea leaves. The letters swim on the page like that and I swim along.

My lap begins with a pronoun and I touch upon Smith at the end. Smith swims well because he keeps up with me on the pages. He finds a way to mirror my moves and we become one in the nakedness of the pages.

Today, I feel like I am becoming Smith.

#2

Dec 3, 2016

12:16 A.M.

The day I learnt that it was acceptable to start a sentence with *but* changed me. There was comfort in knowing that you can start where you left off and not always in the same breath. That you can pause for a full stop, a second longer than what a comma allows. That it is okay to breathe and start over. That it is okay to discontinue and begin anew. That it is okay to pause; to suspend in doubt; to breathe before another lap.

I am in no hurry.

But that is a lie. I am in a hurry. Aren't we all?

Aren't we all just looking for ways to keep ourselves busy before the next existential crisis strikes us and we buckle? So, we hide it in tired forearms holding onto handles keeping us from falling as we travel days and nights and sometimes years in the local. We hide those moments behind laptop screens crunching numbers for a corporation or writing stories that, maybe, were never ours to tell - but that is another kind of crisis and I will be revisiting that many times. We also hide it behind reticent smiles on a Thursday and drinks on a Friday, knowing that the weekend is here and we are ours again, at least for a while. We hide it behind consequent hangovers and 2 minute cigarette breaks, because the smoke makes it difficult to see, anyway. We also hide them behind Facebook cover photos with Schopenhauer's quotes because he can't see those anyway...

So, we reduce him to pixels on a screen, to establish our coolness and maybe we become that too... Cool... Cold... Unfeeling and blind, to the reality of the screen looking at us, when we log in to wish someone a happy birthday. Because days matter. Time matters. We must not pause. We must move. 25 and without a job. Oh my! 23 and no boyfriend. Oh my, you prude! You see, we cannot pause...

So, we stay busy and ignore the fact that maybe, we can pause. Maybe, like grammar, we can fracture life and pause; and take that trip to the hills because we want to pause and not escape.

Maybe, we can and someday we will. Someday we will know the difference between a hammock and a cocoon. But before that time finds me, I will look at Smith and let the tidal wave of envy engulf me - for all the things he doesn't know - for all the things I will never let him know - for all the things, he will never have to see - for all the things he would never dream...

Do I wish I could do that for myself? Hell, yes!

But for now, knowing that Smith is unaware, is enough. As for me, I knew all that time in the library, was going to bite me in the ass someday.

⁂

...WE HIDE IT IN
TIRED FOREARMS
HOLDING ONTO
HANDLES
KEEPING US
FROM FALLING...

Dec 26, 1999

Dearest EB,

You know I have not been the man I was since I first held you in my arms. Let me also tell you that I have not been the man I used to be since your mother first let me hold her. We had been together for 13 years before we finally had you. I know you blame yourself for her leaving us. But for an angel to be born, one had to go back into heaven. You see, that is how balance works.

For your 8th birthday, you wanted a picnic in Fairmount Park. We did that.

The little precocious wonder that you are, you wanted to go to Rodin's Museum on your 9th birthday. We did that, too.

For your 10th birthday, you wanted to climb the Rocky steps and we did. Later in the night, you told me that you wanted to do what I loved. How many times have you snuggled into my bed late into the night (school night, mind you) to watch Apollo Creed and Rocky Balboa beat each other? But they become friends. You see, Elixir, balance finds a way into our lives. Like an angel, balance comes and goes but in that minute of departure, another comes right back, too.

Before you give me your wish list for your 11th birthday,

EB, I want to give you a song your mother used to sing to you when you were nestled in her womb. She wrote the song and asked me to play the guitar when her belly swelled way too much for her to hold it properly. My gift to you is this guitar that she painted with her hands when she could not play it. And the song she sang to you.

Play it on the recorder but hold those tears that I know you will cry, in your palm. I promise one day we will make paper boats float in those tears. We will create new memories. Happier memories.

The tape is enclosed in the envelope. One day when she was not noticing, I recorded her singing it. It is not completely original but she always found a way to own things.

Like my heart and our home.

There is something else in the backyard, too. One gift for my pre-teen is too little.

How are you growing up so fast, EB? I realised that there are things we still have to do. So, starting tomorrow, we will. Starting tomorrow, I will find a way to fix balance into our lives. I am sorry I am away for work but I am grateful that you understand… I am sorry that our home is not as pretty as your friend's, but I am grateful that you try with your fridge magnets and drawings on the wall.

I am sorry that your mother is not with us but I am grateful that you have kept her alive in your eyes and that dimple on the right side of your cheek. And also, your honeycomb hair.

I am sorry that I have not taught you how to ride a bike

but I am grateful for your patience.

Tomorrow, we start.

I promise to hold on till you can fly. I also promise that I will still hold on when you need me to even though you know how to fly.

Happy birthday, baby girl. Please do not grow up so fast.

Also, let's watch Rocky, tonight?

With all my love and the one you will find hidden in the skies above, behind a star you named after her,

Your Pa

PS- I will be home after despatching the next order of books. I sneaked in one edition for you.

It is right under your pillow.

The song: *for those who want to read(/ri:d/) it-*

When I was young, My mother sang to me
Que Sera Sera as we sat in the shade of a tree
but I will add to it, a little symphony-
Que Sera Sera darling, because you will always find me;
Holding you when you take your first walk;
Looking over your shoulder when you write your first letter;
Holding the brush with you every time you create art;
You will always find me
in the home in your heart.

When I was young, My father sang to me
Butterfly kisses as we cycled to the beach
but I will add to it another symphony-
Butterfly kisses are what I will need;
But I will give you butterfly wings to fly
and a sky to find as you dream;
You will fly for I will be your gravity;
I will let you fly
while waiting by the beach.

When I was young, we sang 100 miles as a family;
But I will add yet another symphony-
When you find your way,
walk on.
But when you look back;
We will be right where you left us for this journey;

Looking over your shoulder when you wrote your first letter;
Holding the brush with you every time you created art;
You will always find your family
In the home you built in our hearts.

#3
Dec 3, 2016
12:50 A.M.

Faucet.
Facet.
Face it.
Face.

These words appeared in my dreams multiple times last night or this morning. It is hard to keep a count of numbers when you are sleeping. I could never understand that sheep game anyway.

Does it bore you to sleep? Or keep you awake to keep a track? Are numbers always boring? I don't know. They have their own dance and alphabets dance along. What is the difference in writing 1 and one? But the book cover always says Three Cups of Tea while the third page is marked as 3. What is the difference?

In faces and in faucets.

They leak the same way.

Faucet. Facet. Face it. Face.

These words could have contributed to making a great poem, maybe. But there are conditions. It would have to be written by someone who has a shitty background and is suicidal and then the world will take it seriously. Maybe, Bukowski. But then he was too lazy to kill himself and I am too busy living life on pages and making some on screen.

Who will take my poetry seriously?

Who will my words matter to?

Are they too soppy or soft?

But that is what happens to one's face when water hits it.

That is what is happening to the clay around the rink in the basin with the leaking faucet.

Its fading. Eroding.

The water tank is finishing.

I am bathing in trickles and coming out with soap suds still in my brown hair.

I always wanted highlights, anyway. The towel is enough for today.

The plumber can wait.

I am not yet done with this facet of my life, or this faucet in my bathroom or let's face it, this life and his face. He came into my dreams last night along with these names.

The plumber will just have to wait.

Because even with soap on my palms and probably hiding in my uncombed hair I am interested in writing.

I know I am seconds from typing when I hear the tapping. So, the plumber will just have to wait while the faucet falls into my palms rolls into my fingers and drips onto a keyboard.

I will swim on the screen with words and numbers, headers and footers.

For today, that is enough.

⁕

FAUCET.
FACET.
FACE IT.
FACE.

CHAPTER 3

She runs her fingers over the screen sometimes. I think she clears the dust off the screen but Smith believes she tries to touch me or us or him. The lines are blurring, now. Smith feels like home, now.

He has finite answers for me. He is becoming someone I like.

Also, he believes things I will like to believe.

So, the touch is warm. It feels nice. It feels warm. She is warm, too.

She looks intently at the screen creating a world that she dreams of in the wee hours of the morning. She reserves them for me. And Smith. And it is nice. We like being the first waking thought she has.

Sometimes, Smith rests on the screen but we go on a walk. She walks by the sea and we talk. Like old times. Before Smith. But unlike before, I do not have answers for her. I only have more questions. Smith has become the answers.

Both of us pirouette around the beach and find ourselves in front of the screen. I hide in the folds of her fingers as she presses key after key and Smith appears to answer her questions and sometimes, mine.

So, today I learnt that I like café latte from Starbucks in Callowhill Street especially when it is hot enough to deceive me under the froth. I lick it off my frosted lips and my tongue becomes eggshell. I know eggshell. I was born somewhere splayed on that colour in the first couple of months.

I also like a face I see in the café. Her name is 'She' for now. I have not spoken to her yet. Smith really wants to. I can wait. I want to hear Elixir first. With Elixir, I feel banked. I think that was Smith talking. I am not funny. But Smith is. She smiles as she writes. Something about this solo guitarist wandering the streets of Philly makes her smile.

She knows me better because of Smith.

I can live with that, too.

#4
Dec 10, 2016
10:07 P.M.

Touch is a strange thing. I remember when I touched myself for the first time. Later, I just knew it was not something kids do- I can almost hear Freud rolling in his grave.

Then, puberty came and along with it, came the obvious awkwardness. But not in my case. I was excited at the prospect of growing up. Of knowing that I needed a bra now even though my boobs felt like mosquito bites swollen because of repeated scratching. So, I was excited at the sight of pubic hair. I knew I was getting bigger and that my body was readying to change and growing. It was the most exciting feeling. And then I leaked for the first time when I was 14. I was peeing when I saw a little red and I grew up a little more again.

Pa was gone by then and my aunt told me what to do with sanitary napkins.

All the girls in my school used tampons but my aunt had a problem with the idea.

"It is too invasive and you are too young for that."

I was 16 when I touched myself, intentionally, again. I touched myself and I remember it felt moist. That is all I remember from the first time. I am sure my aunt wouldn't want to know this.

She didn't know the life I had, anyway. So, I let her think I was young. She did not know my singer-songwriter boyfriend who I gave all my pocket money coins to, while he played Tom Waits and Damien Rice. She would not even know the one singer-songwriter who actually mattered. Tom Cash. Thomas. But he was too hipster to sound Victorian and I too much in love, to argue – the one who sang Cliff Richard and touched me like never before. First, my knee, then my wrist... Then something in my stomach churned and my head was light when his forehead was on my lips. He went lower and something below my stomach churned this time. He was my first.

Touch has always intrigued me. I had submitted a piece on 'touch' on my friend's blog, because I went around touching everything to feel it. The paints on my desk, CD covers, the dust on walls, Ginnie's nails, the seats of my car, the keyboard before I typed...

This is one of the pieces I am not ashamed of. I am sure my aunt would be if she read it. I remember it. It is open on the screen as I touch the pen to leak on paper. Moving through the poetic and the prosaic. My journal entries are messy.

Stream of consciousness? I would like to believe that, but also because it is true. I write this journal before I set out to type. This journal helps me collect my thoughts.

This journal touches my thoughts.
So touch and the blog.

The piece is titled SKIN.

Don't get me wrong,
I like touch.
I like the idea of touch.
I like being touched.

Like the canvas that touches my paint streaked finger;
I like a hesitant touch like that.
Wait. Premeditate. Give up. Surrender.
I like that touch.

Like hands that brush accidentally during walks;
Wildly swinging arms colliding to cause a spark the intensity of star dust.
I like touching the dust.
I like that touch.

Like fingers that touch upon electronic letters to write;
Write when what I actually do, is type.
The touch lets me believe that the crawling ants on the screen are mine
I like that touch.

Like the eyelash bending ever so often to feel the eyelid separated from it by my stare;
The touch that is incomplete in aim but complete in pursuit;

A touch that is an endeavour.
I like that touch.

Like the coffee that cannot stay away from the skin of my thigh and spills when my phone vibrates
It leaves me warm when I don't want it.
So, I throw water on it and sigh
But warmth is good.
And I like what the touch tries.

Like the same coffee that touches dried lips and burns the tongue;
The froth deceiving the hot milk beneath
A touch that pains a third.
Touch that travels.
I like that touch

'Pa tells me when I was an infantile victim of January cold, I would snuggle up to him to feel warm.'
That touch taught me warmth.
I like that touch.

Like the wet remnants of hands touching each other;
The sweat makes you slip yours off my palm.
We laugh because our fingers still linger.
Eyelashes over eyelids.
A touch that is obstructed.
I like that touch.

Like the bottle that surrenders to my lips;
Every time I want to get a little buzzed
It touches my mind and I dance to celebrate this communion.
We touch.

Like a hug that tells me that holding on feels good;
Arms that refuse to leave but feet that evacuate.
A touch that wants to be as much as it wants to leave.
Eyelashes over eyelids.
I like that touch.

'Pa tells me, when I was a toddler and a little too cute,
I would run away from cuddles claiming an absolute lack of breath only to return for some more.'
I knew warmth in that touch - I found home.
I tell Pa that I touched a hand on a street - a tiny hand that splayed its tinier fingers to accommodate more than her palm allowed, that wanted money but only got a warm hand from me.
She smiled and I saw warmth simmering in a familiar home.
Life travels,
And so, does touch.
And that is why I like the idea of skin,

and what it does.

So, I touch upon the keyboard and create. I have never touched Smith, though, but he feels more real than those around me. Maybe because I create him with every word. Maybe, each word touches him.

Poetic to the prosaic. This journal will be one hell of a confusing read for the one who tries, if he/she tries. But right now, I am trying.

⁂

CHAPTER 4

Some days, we go to a Café. People are stacked one on top of the other and the music makes it impossible to hear what the other is thinking, let alone the sound of their muffled breath. I cannot even hear the sound of the keys when her fingers touch the keyboard. I wonder why she chooses this place.

We used to go to quiet places before where she could hear my questions and where she could answer them.

Now she goes to a place where she cannot hear me anymore.

I go along because I like seeing. Not that I have much of a choice. I go along wherever she takes me. I saw someone who looked like me, Smith, the other day. He was wearing a white shirt and blue jeans. He was also carrying a tan bag, though I do not think he left it at the cafe. We left before he did.

I do not know if she noticed but there he was. Smith like I have known.

We still go on walks and I see people I would like to be - like the person who shops like there is no tomorrow. The glint in his eye is more inviting than the pool of bags swarming his arms. He knows what will look good on his body. He covers his nakedness with that. I do not even know if I am naked anymore. Because Smith wears a white shirt today too but with cargo pants. So, my nakedness of hollowness between arched letters is now clothed. I want to be able to choose what I want to wear too. Like that man with the shopping bags.

There is also this one person we see who loves to run. I remember when I ran across pages and lines like that, oscillating between pronouns and Smith. Now, I hear myself and see myself in every line. Every syllable that rolls off her pink tongue, falls on my floating frame and I swim on the page of the text. I do not run anymore because there is no space. Smith and I are one and this is our story.

Only we do not know it yet.

I almost feel like her. Living my day without knowing what it will be like. Living my day as it unfolds before me - not knowing.

I become Smith and he is me, now. I do not mind it at all. In Smith are all the answers even if he does not know them yet. We move around pages and somewhere in the dog ears and the ink stains in her journal, we find the answers.

They are hidden in the page behind the curve where

the name Smith lurks and she scratches out 'he' and writes it. I have a name, now. I am not interchangeable anymore. I move along pages, along cafes, along the sea as Smith and I can live with that.

For now.

And for some more time, I think.

I like it here.

I MOVE ALONG THE PAGES,
ALONG CAFES, ALONG THE
SEA AS SMITH AND I CAN
LIVE WITH THAT.

#5
Dec 11, 2016
10:15 A.M.

I'm sitting outside an engineering college in Malad waiting to go to Kandivali West-It took me a long time to pronounce it correctly to the Cab driver and he took me all over the blue thatched roofs and blackening doors of Malad to Borivali, with chickens peeping out of windows with nothing to do but wait- I am still learning the restrained 'r', the open 'a' and the 'v' that lasts just a second. My own name sounds weird resting on an alien tongue here. X sounds more like J and I become alien to the sound of my own name. I respond, nonetheless because I have stopped correcting Lal Ji from my building and the *bhaiya-s* who sell tomatoes and carrots that suit the pasta I make; that Shanti Didi cleans as she wakes me up at 7 a.m.

Elixir (with a J) *Didi, durwaaza kholo.*

So, I have been re-christened as I moved to Malad East, Park Regency, #1402. I have become Elixir with an 'e' formed by parting lips only too eager to meet the tongue to touch 'l' and hide behind teeth to make 'i' and then strike against them to make 'j' replace the 'x', flatten into an 'i' and close together to make the final 'r' that does not roll on the tongue but stays benched behind one's teeth between the little space under the tongue and the lower jaw. That is my name in Bombay... Mumbai. As convoluted as the lanes that brought me to this college. We went up a slope and I remembered my summer in San Francisco with its undulating roads and accelerating slopes. Just that this San Francisco is different than what the Animals dreamt of and this one smells different. It is new to me and old to everyone around me. So, my surprise is 'bleh' to them. They wonder how these slopes and vendors can interest me. I think they think of me as Julia Roberts from Eat Pray Love and I am laughing inside with this parallel. I always wanted to be a solo traveller to India but I had never hoped of becoming a Hollywood fetish. Am I the fetish or am I fetishising? Anyway, these roads lead me to a college and I wonder again what I am doing here.

There is nothing engineered about this place though.

There are crows flying above my head and autos stopping by hoping I will take one of them. They slow down as they close in on the lamp post I'm leaning my back against. I decline with a smile.

They don't smile back. No one smiles around here. Not the *auto-wallas* (walla shows belonging. Shanti Didi told me so. It's a nice word). Not even the crows. Not even the dogs wagging their tails and chasing each other. They might end up having sex. These two. And even they aren't smiling. They remind me of a couple that stays next to my apartment in Park Regency. I chose it because it has trees. A little green for the grey. 50 shades of green for a million greys - in hair, in walls, in palms and in hearts. Anyway, I hear them make love sometimes. I can't help it. The walls are thin. I don't want to but I can't help it. The favourite spot in my apartment meets their wall. So, while I type I hear moans and groans. A little sigh, a massive gasp for my tak tak tak. But they don't smile. Not in the morning. Not when I head out to pick up the paper and meet her eye. She doesn't smile. Not at me. Not at the milk in her hands. Not at the reflection of herself she catches in the mirror placed between the elevators. It helps me when I'm rushing out and have to pirouette to see if everything is in place. The surface agrees and the reflection smiles at me. That is enough sometimes. A smile outside the four walls of my home. Ginnie smiles all the time and I'm used to it now.

So the *auto-wallas* don't smile. They leave with the *creechhhhh* of their autos. My earphones forget what they were playing for that moment. But they always stop. 5 have stopped already.

Clearly, they don't think the honeycomb of my hair belongs here. They would rather take me to an art gallery in Kala Ghoda.

A kid, probably 13,with thin hair covering the skin above his upper lip just looked at me questioningly.

His younger brother looked on too.

Someone in a burka walked up to me and asked my name. I could only see eyes. They are the easiest to respond to. Pitch black with specs of chocolate floating in the centre. So, I told her.

All of them think I'm lost.

But I'm not. I know exactly where I am.

I don't think my 1500/- worth of Fab India maxi that I got from that advance that finished in 3 days belongs on a pavement that people sleep on.

But that's the thing. I belong here more than in front of the portraits in Jehangir Art Gallery.

They tell me nothing about the person.

But just about the stares... They have beautiful telling eyes too, but it stops there.

Here, reclining against this lamp post that is stronger than my back, in the uncomfortable lack of my presence, I learn a world of these people. And no Heidegger, It's not the world of the Peasant's Shoes. It is simpler than that.

It is a world of shitting in the open while having sex under sheets.

It's a world of buying sanitary napkins in black bags but shouting cunt out loud.

It's a world where lovers make out in the open but buy condoms from a store at least 1km from where they live.

It's the world of lives lived in autos and laughs heard outside.

It's the world where I wait on pavements before I, childless, am going to talk to people about parenting correctly. *Gauge your child's education.*

What was my friend even thinking when he asked me to join him?

I think he asked because the others said no.

Anyway, I still have to learn about the city and any movement helps. So, I move along this world with this journal and a dream from last night with me.

I want to type again, but I'm heading to a place I don't know for answering questions I don't have answers to. I don't even have questions for this world.

It's a world where these hormonal children look at my honeycombed hair as though a bee puked on it just a minute ago and they were around to catch that magic.

It's a world where I'm still waiting for my friend to come while I sit in an unexplored part of Mumbai. Me - outside an engineering college. Waiting... Never thought this could happen, but stranger things have happened. Like looking for faces.

I am doing the same, now. Still looking for one. It's a friend's this time. But it's still a face and I look on. I have seen many on the 5 red buses that have crossed me. They look out of the window while I look at them. We meet and, in that moment, all of us have a collective story. That's the world, Heidegger but that Ola cab with my friend is still not here and he is still not looking out of the window as I look into every cab that crosses. And I look on.

And for now, I'm pissed.

A kid just spat a pool of his mucous 10 steps away from my feet. A crow flies above this pool, almost diving into it and I cringe and look away. The dog and the bitch are copulating. The chase is over. She barks and I see her spit dissipating in the air around.

I am almost sure someone pooped 10 yards away from me. I can smell it.

But I can vaguely smell roses too because I am close to a mosque. A green flag flying with the same crows tells me that and a sound from a microphone confirms my doubts.

There is a tap here too, but it does not leak till someone uses it. 5 people have used it before me. One man with a grizzly beard and grizzlier feet washed them under the tap. It trickled for 2 seconds after he closed it. A little girl washed her hands after falling on the ground. She looked okay with the fall, just worried about the dirt splashed on her clothes and hands. A woman with greying hair washed the grime off her face under the same tap as she disembarked from the bus that left 2 minutes ago. It was red. What a colour for a bus! Not a bright red, a rusting red and at night you can see the blue of the lights against the red. There was another kid who washed his hair under the tap. He was shirtless, just in his underpants and one fifth the size of the pillar holding the banner of the college... The fifth one was me. I just opened it to hear it. And to hear the trailing leakage that stopped after 2 seconds.

*

#6
Dec 15, 2016
12:45 P.M.

I don't know what I did in Kandivali West or what my friend was trying. I could not write about the face of the one I dreamt of nor the story. All I know is that I left my bag there and I need it back.

Smith, the character, from my book does the same and he is always with me.

Did I leave my bag because I have become Smith while obsessing over him or was it an honest mistake?

All I know is I had to make the horrible trip back to the place in the sweltering heat to retrieve my bag. Everything was the same. The dogs were still there, the crows were still flying, the passers-by still looked on questioningly and I could smell roses.

My bag was there. Smith and I found our bags and I carried mine home.

1:30 P.M.

I don't know what to do with Smith anymore. I was once told, ask your character and he will lead you. But that does not work. Smith with his wheatish face gleaming at the nose with hair parted on the left and a growing stubble just looks at me waiting for me to tell him what to do.

I don't know.

Does he have a job?

Does he have a girlfriend?

Was he abused as a child?

Did he paint a wall in Philly with his pee?

Does he smoke? Does he smoke up?

Does he like whiskey or wine?

If wine, then tannic or sweet? Red or white?

There is too much to know and I don't know where we are going.

I don't know where Smith is going.

But we are going somewhere.

2:20 P.M.

I am in the local train from Goregaon to Churchgate. There is a separate compartment for women and that is supposed to make me feel safe. No one knows that I carry Smith with me. In my head.

Will they mind if they knew? I don't think they'd care.

3:30 P.M.

I am standing in front of Jehangir Art Gallery. There was a time I loved these galleries. I even wrote on art. Ekphrastic poetry, my art history teacher said, is soul for the canvas.

I was naive so I believed in his romanticism. I even wrote one of my own.

It was called Questions and was on a blog that my friend ran. The blog was called 'Musings' and I was one of the Muses on the blog. Lame, I know. But I was young and in love with life and everything it offered. So.

Questions
- Elixir Banks
16.07.2009

To - Rene Magritte
From- A Smoker

If a pipe is not a pipe,
Then are you Rene?
or are you Magritte?
Am I here or am I there?
Am I in Virginia's room or Descartes'?
When the walls of Delphi shout out Know Thyself, who is this 'thy' I have to know?

Tell me Magritte, because you made me question the Cuban in my hand.
Do I also question the smoke?

I cannot stand galleries with their blank portraits anymore. They tell me nothing about the person on the canvas or behind it. I am left questioning and wondering weaving stories in my head. And Smith gets confused with these portraits. I know he does. I can tell.

Who knows him better than I do? There is too much ambiguity in blank stares and now, I cannot take it. I want intensity to replace this ambiguity. I want Smith to replace these blank stares.

6:30 P.M.

I am sitting in Café Mondegar. Miranda sure knows how to decorate walls with people. But there are people all around. People sitting on chairs around tables talking, uncaring. People serving with polite smiles and glistening kindness and people on the walls having their own party. The walls in Philly weren't like this. They were colourful, yes. But they were colours. These are people. And too many.

I am swimming in them. And Smith swims along.

I order a Kingfisher and stir it even though it's not needed. Something about the 'whoosh' of this swirl comforts me and maybe, Smith. And now I am going to type amidst this pool of humanity that I have become a part of.

I am drowning in their voices but drowning is good because I struggle to hear myself in the noise and the struggle makes my voice louder. It makes Smith's voice louder.

And for now, that is enough.

⁂

Ce n'est pas un livre

CHAPTER 5

Today, I am wearing a black shirt and olive green pants. I, Smith, have changed for the night. I do not forget my bag in strange places anymore either. I carry it with me all along. Smith and I are one. I ensure he does not leave his bag astray and he ensures that I hide my nakedness.

Yes, today, Smith and I are one.

We move through pronouns and proper nouns as one. Our hands move along pages as she writes. Her caresses are ours and the wine she drank last night is ours to taste.

I, Smith, am reddened at the eggshell of my being and we see life coming in.

Sometimes, I like the idea of moving the distance from the screen to the desk and beyond, but my hands are splayed holding the page open for her to write on. It is when she writes that we are one, too.

#7
Dec 16, 2016
11:45 P.M.

I read The Little Prince, again. And not the whole book just the first couple of pages about the boa constrictor. And I thought about Chugtai's Lihaf.

We hide a little too much, don't we?

I know I do.

Shanti Didi doesn't know where I am from.

I never told Tom. He came to know on his own.

Lal Ji doesn't know that men stay over-harmless backpackers or friends of friends.

But men.

Smith doesn't know anything, really.

Freddie doesn't know why I wouldn't come back.

Redford doesn't know I am writing and getting published.

I think it's just this journal that knows. A lot.

A strange combination of papers and glue that I talk to. That listens and never talks back. Like one of those professional therapists I was forced to see after Pa left.

So maybe strangers are easier to talk to. You won't see them again. Maybe, you won't even talk again. So, they leave with a part of your world with them hidden behind receding hairlines and breast pockets, fingerprints on lighters or one less cigarette in their packet, less sleep hijacked by conversations and the feeling of another of one's kind in the strive of being different, unique, distinct. They leave but they carry you with them. Does that mean they are still strangers? Maybe, familiar but still strangers.

Familiar strangers.

That can be the title of my next book.

⁂

From: Freddie Reynold <F.Reynold@timeconsultancy.in>
Date: Fri, Dec 17, 2016 at 12:09 AM
Subject: Hey kid!
To: elixir.banks3@gmail.com

EB,

What are you doing so far away from home? Your last mail scared the shit out of me!

Bud, Come back? Edgar Allan Poe is waiting for you by Delaware. Just come back, you.

I cannot take those reunion parties without you. Remember dancing to Larger than Life?

I want that back, no one here knows the steps. They try to be you but you know no one can.

Come back, yo! Your home is here. Everything is the same. I got Uncle Banks' photo framed and put it over the TV like you told me too. Can you please stop feeling guilty for not spending enough time with him before he left us for good? You did not know, EB. Stop punishing yourself.

Your fridge magnet with the photo of your first cycle is still there. And that stupid painting we made together in your room is still there on the fridge. It is a house with memories. You love memories, you stupid hoarder. Come back and we will make more.

Emails. We never even texted. We just knocked on each other's doors.

I miss the sound of your peculiar knock.

Tap tapatap-tapataptaptap.

I want to hear it, again. Okay, I am done cribbing and lunch hour is over so I better get back to fixing accounts for a person I don't know because that is my life, now.

I promise that was the last crib.

This is just a rant from a friend who is missing his partner in crime too much. I know you need time. But stop feeling guilty!! What happened with Tom will not define the rest of your life. He is happy, he has moved on. Stop killing yourself over things that the past holds. Leave it at a stupid nostalgia shop. But for now, do what you want to do because you won't listen to me, anyway.

Even though I miss you and want you back this minute.

At least, give me your number? So, I can call and pester you.

And McLeod Ganj? What! Are you a hippie backpacking across India, now?

Are you going to meditate and be one with nature, EB?

Shit, I miss making one of my goody-two-shoes wannabe badass moronic child.

Forgive yourself and come back, please.

I miss you.

Love and kicks on your ass,

FR

⁂

#8
Dec 17, 2016
5:00 A.M.

I have not slept all night because I have been reading a friend's blog. A blog I had submitted a poem to as a 17 year old. I cringe at my words and their dishonesty now but they were real, then.

Because I was in love. That Crimson Crunch love benched on a stubble.

ADVERTISEMENTS
- Elixir Banks
14. 04. 2005

We were not like others. We did not reserve the weekends for our words. We were different from others. We chose sleepy Monday mornings instead.

'We have a story'
No we don't. We could have but you never let it happen.
Our story sits in a book with a cover I designed. With a title I decided.
But with pages you never filled.
So, it has a prologue but no body.
And I'm too hopeful to write the epilogue, just yet
So, we don't have a story. We have episodes. Episodes of touch and miss with advertisements longer than the actual show.

Advertisements of your Marlboro and my Sultry Pink;
Advertisements of your Jack Daniel and my Jamaican;
Advertisement of your recklessness and my caution;
Advertisement of your extreme indifference and my concern.
Advertisements that go on and on and force you to change the channel. But you always find your way back to know what the rest of the 'story' holds for you.
So, we are not in the pages of a book. We are on the screen of a TV.
We are not held together like pages of a book but are distinct like the pixels on a screen.
We are not even us, just separate entities.

I want us in a book without a bookmark. I want us in a library on the topmost rack so no one can see.
I want us in the forbidden section so no one knows. I want us in a corner that even the librarian doesn't see.

So,
Your words, let them be mine...
My name, I'll let you sign.
Be my cover.
Bound together.
Stay.
Smell like the pages of an old book
And I swear I'll read you all day.

The blog still has my name and a few excited teenagers' comments.

'Oh! I love the smell of old books', says xoxo3.

'I think you have a story if he made you write this,' says, 4eva16.

'Move on, you. You can write poems. You are way cooler than him,' says, leo3

'Let us make a story? ;),' says coolguy93.

I cringe with the knowledge of my own stupidity and the Sula helps forget it.

I have been listening to the faucet and that is the only music I know. I feel Ginnie at my feet and she is the only warmth I feel. But I look at the screen and my words and the comments that followed and I feel deceived.

6:30 A.M.

I have not slept all night and now Ginnie squirms at my feet.

The screen has been open for a while but I have not written. I think Smith is sleeping.

8:00 A.M.

Ginnie and I returned from a morning walk. I got a leash so she does not run off scared, anymore.

I am holding her bicycle and she knows she is balanced.

I walked down the freshly wet roads of Malad.

There are apartments that rise up to 17 floors or more.

The sun does not let me look beyond 17 and I never really cared about numbers.

So, we walked past the apartment, the vendors, the chemist shop where I buy condoms from and always get strange looks (I am still getting a grasp of the culture of this place), the parlour where I get my brows threaded. She always compliments my fair skin but tells me I have dark circles. I once told her I have trouble sleeping because of a leaking faucet and she gave me a plumber's card. I threw it in the bin along with the astringent soaked cotton. We walked towards Goregaon next. We saw chickens as they waited for death to come and we saw other dogs look at Ginnie knowing that it will find her too, soon. She is old, this one. We have been together a long time.

They looked at her and I looked at them and for once, I was glad, Ginnie couldn't see.

I bummed a smoke while Ginnie waited. I only allow myself one smoke a day and this was the perfect time for I was celebrating. I was celebrating for Smith.

For once, I am glad that Smith can only see what I want him to see.

And for now that is enough.

So he will see hills when we leave for McLeod Ganj tomorrow. It is a long way up but I know it is worth it. I know it because that stubbed- cheek- leaking- faucet-face told me of his McLeod adventures and I know I will find answers for my wheatish- complexion, left parted hair-growing stubble Smith, there.

For now, knowing answers are not far, is enough.

We will get there.

⁂

SMELL LIKE THE PAGES OF AN OLD BOOK
AND I SWEAR I'LL READ YOU ALL DAY.

CHAPTER 6

We do not go for walks now. We stay in the hills. The only hills I knew were pages stacked up in an ignored pile from where I escaped to be written about again.

I remember my first excursion to the bin and back.

She was disappointed and annoyed. The phone rang and she was angry. She picked up a pile of me before I was Smith and threw me, the potential Smith, in the bin. I crept from behind the discarded papers as the 'he' she wrote about. That night she picked up another page and a new pen. I was baptized that day. I became new. She rolled me up in a joint and smoked me onto a page. I tasted the spilled wine on the pages and knew what she tasted like in that instant.

We became new in that moment.

I have never been on an excursion since - just a trip around the bookmark or the tent of a dog ear in her journal. On the screen, I am intact.

I take a break when she is tired. We understand

each other like that.

But never another excursion like that one.

Now, we move together. Her, Smith and I as an indomitable trinity, we move through the sea and the seaside knowing that we will meet at the intersection of a page and screen.

Today, we sit together looking into the valley. She looks on and I see what it is like. It is fragrant and smells of pine. At least that is what she thinks. I nod along because I know Smith would do that. I understand Smith, now. He nods when she needs to hear a yes. He does not throw the ambiguous questions I threw at her. Smith understands her and so do I, now.

At least I try to. Smith helps me with that.

So, I nod along, now.

Pines, yes.

I hope she will have wine before coming to me, too.

Then I will know what she smells like and what she tastes like.

I will know things too. Like Smith.

That will be nice.

#9
Dec 18, 2016
19:45 P.M.

I don't like the hills. It has been a week. I wish I was like Smith. I wish I could live time across pages on a screen. Jumping through seconds and minutes in a colossal duet, one paragraph at a time. The length of the paragraph can be small or big depending on how much love I find in it. But that is not how I live. Stupid science and relativity and all that crap that I never really understood in school. So, I have to stay here for 3 more days because I have paid from an already diminishing account.

Smith is weird here too. He does not talk. I have a feeling I am losing him to the echo.

I think he likes it here.

Does he not care that I hate it?

I hate it.

I can't stand the hills. I want to go back to the sea.

To the apartment where I am called Elixir with a J for an X. Go back to Ginnie. I am worried that Carol is not taking good care of my baby. Carol cannot take care of herself let alone my baby. What was I thinking! I trusted a person I met at a bar a week ago with my love!

But I am lonely and Smith can only talk so much. After a while he is quiet and Carol does not shut up. She wants me to meet someone. She goes on and on about it. Sometimes she is loud enough to drown the voices of other's. She is no Freddie. But she will do, for now.

So, I am going back home in 72 hours and 36 minutes and 33 seconds to be precise. 32 seconds now.

That is how futile time is. It changes the minute I mention it and still we hold on to it with all our strength. (I will probably use this line in the book).

And Smith is not quietened in the leaking faucet. I hear the *tak tak tak* and *tip tip tip* just fine.

We will go back and he will come back to me.

Just knowing that is enough.

Bloody Smith. At least I know he can't run away from me.

⁂

I HAVE A FEELING I AM LOSING HIM TO THE ECHO.

CHAPTER 7

Becoming one was easy. I think I was Smith, always. It is easier to know who you are when someone else tells you who you are. Maybe that is why her trip to the retreat in the hills failed. There was no one to tell her who she was.

But then she came back and there I was. Smith. I answer her questions-to tell her that she carried the lingering smell of pine in her hair and that she always smelled of cigarettes and red wine. I could tell her that, but I'm sure she knows already.

I know myself better, too. I like wine, apparently. I also like the idea of long walks. I am too immersed in thoughts to care about bags and clothes and maybe, that is the reason I do not bother changing. I am still in the same white shirt and the blue jeans. I think this combination has become my skin now. I know myself through it. Maybe the clothes are my nakedness. Everything before that was covered. I was just letters, now I am a form that breathes into the gaping holes in between the curves of the letters. Earlier, I swam on the page. Now I float, effortlessly in the white of my own shirt and blue waves of my own jeans.

Today, I left a job because it stopped making sense to me. She said, ''Do you want to be stuck or do you want to move on?"

I remembered running through pages and realised that I cannot stay. I like moving through pronouns and proper nouns, through lisping Ss and pursing Ms. So, we moved along with the ever forgotten bag slung over the floating shoulder of my form. We did not leave it somewhere. Now it comes with me wherever I go.

She asked, "Do you want to leave it here?" I remembered how I hated when Smith left it loose. He did not feel like me. So, we carry it now wherever we go. This is the Smith I can be. And she lets me be.

I can live with that.

She asked me, "Where do we move from here?"

I remembered thinking how the journey from one page to the next was enough to know a little more.

But today, we moved back to the first page. We travelled back in time. It only makes sense to revisit what was, to know what will be.

That was the time I did not know Smith. That was the time I did not know I was Smith.

That was the time of abandoned bags and wine spills. The page still smells of it. And I am there too, lying somewhere between a mess of vowels and consonants carrying that smell in me, in the breast pocket of my white shirt - the one I wore at the beginning? Remember that?

#10
Dec 19, 2016
11:50 P.M

As a kid, I always saw people as colours. Always. I feel the same way now. After all these years. It could be because of the class I am taking, *Chakras and Aura* while still in McLeod. But I think I always saw people as colours. I simply forgot.

Pa was yellow- a leaked droplet of sunshine walking on earth to make days happy and nights warm.

Mum, I always imagined as pink. I always had and still have a picture of my parents back at our home in Philly of the time they were pregnant with me. Pa said it is our family photo - that behind the pink camisole, I was safely cocooned. Or hammocked. So, Mum is pink. It suits her.

Tom was Cobalt Teal - the colour of Santorini- with the wave of comfort he brought into my life. I was whole again when the sky and the ocean met and blurred. He was the kind of blue that left me smiling.

I guess, he thinks of me as black.

Poe was always red. Always.

Freddie is orange. Redford was emerald. Aunt was grey. Carol is violet. Shanti is purple like the twilight. Lal Ji is brown.

Ginnie is yellow because she is my last living memory of Pa. She carries the streaks of his sunshine.

But Smith, is white.

- a blank paper

- blinding light
- milk that I hate
- whipped cream that I love
- a blank canvas
- the tips of my nails
- the strings of my uke
- my bedroom walls
- my earphones
- Ginnie's eyes

Maybe, if he hits a prism, he might break into Freddie's orange, Redford's emerald, Pa's yellow, Mum's pink, Tom's Blue, Aunt's grey and Poe's red.

⁂

Objective To find Smith

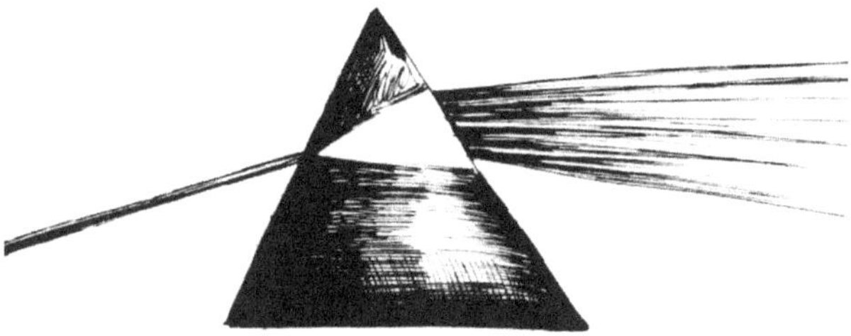

Materials required

Pa's yellow
Ma's pink
Vixen's emerald
Fred's orange
Tom's blue
Poe's red
Aunt's grey
Pink Floyd's record

Riya

Dec 21
Dear EB,

Is it time to say goodbye to Ginnie already? Thanks for your apartment. I am sure you would not mind if I told you I was not alone on all nights. Hah! Gotcha!

So, like I promised, I didn't bring anyone to your apartment.

Along with Ginnie, I was a good girl too.

Now, I am going back from the sabbatical.

Call me when you read this. I know you are a hoarder so I am leaving this post it on the mirror, here. ☺

Call me! I have stuff to tell you. And let's make a plan for your birthday?

Hugs,
-Carol

PS - Thanks for all the wine.

#11
Dec 23, 2016
12:00 A.M.

I have just come back from this godforsaken Fiction Workshop. Everything I write, is 'not enough'.

Apparently, my character does not make sense to them. They want to know more. How can I tell them when I don't know? I don't even know what kind of music I want to write to anymore.

So, I just leave the radio on. Now the faucet and music run in the absence of my control. I let them drip.

Sometimes my eyes leak with frustration, too.

There is another kind of frustration. I don't even want to dwell on it. I have not had a man in a while. Not since him.

But now, I have Smith. We go on dates. Just us. I am learning things about him when we walk by Marine Drive. Always at 1:00 A.M. before the police throws us out. It is quiet and the sea sounds better than this faucet. We talk when we sit in Café Mondegar. I am always a little buzzed with the Kingfisher in my hand but he carries me home. Smith is the only man in my life right now.

Pa left trying to teach me balance. Tom left me when I lost my balance.

Now, Smith is holding the back seat of my cycle to support me.

And for now, that will do.

1:00 A.M.

Smith also makes me forget. I forgot what I was writing about. A Fiction Workshop.

So, I got a shitty advance for this book where Smith lives. So, I moved to a place I knew was cheaper. I moved because I could not stand Philly anymore and the proximity of my apartment with the Get Away Café but I tell myself the reasons were monetary and that is easier to handle.

So, the workshop. They want me to write who Smith is.

I almost feel like giving them a character sketch like in school.

"Hamlet was a nice kid whose Hamartia killed him."

But why should I name him. What's in a name? That is all the Shakespeare I know and I have exhausted my knowledge in my journal.

But I know how my name became important to me when Tom changed it. I wrote about it, too. In another journal. I will paste it here. It will make the task of my biographer easier.

While I am being delusional, let me tell you that I think it is half decent. Really. Maybe.

Christened -
You christened me on Monday and I was new.
Someone called me that again. You know how you accidentally changed the last syllable of my name and made me someone else. Someone did just that today.
The word that escaped the corners of your mouth found a home on someone else's tongue.
That person let it out, today.
I gasped.
And then smiled.
I was looking over a book rack when you chose to change my name to call my attention.
Over Tuesdays with Morrie, you changed my Monday.
I was in the library today, too, when someone used that word.
It was while reading Bukowski's words, that I found my word again.
So, the syllable stretched a little too much and a sigh accentuated the tiredness of the stretch.
So, the tiredness mirrored the pining of my hearing ear and the one that silenced it.
So, the ear felt a tremor and the flat line of my lips displaced into a curve.
So, the word that was uttered mindlessly then, came reluctantly back to my world.
Amidst signatures.
Beyond worlds.
Within suppressed giggles.
There it was. Lurking in a voice stained by blotted ink.
There stood my word.

I had stopped posting on the blog because Tom told me it was a stupid place for my talent. Like the GetAway Café for his. But he had to make ends meet so I went along with the hypocrisy and passive sexism.

But I used to like hearing what the kids had to say about my work. Even if they were lame enough to sign off as coolguy93- they were important because they were my readers. I wanted to know what they had to say.

Much like I like to know what Smith has to say.

This is what he has told me so far.

Well, Smith is a tall, lanky guy from Philly. He has a little bit of Italy in him in those dark eyes and the accent he occasionally borrows from his mother. He has sun baked skin and a flick always obscures the right part of his eye or left – we are still deciding. He does not shave every day. He makes up his mind in the morning. Depends on whether he has someone to rub his cheek against or not. His girl, Ebbie, left him for an artist who painted the wall of his favourite house on 7th Street. Now, he leaves his tan bag randomly in places. And runs to retrieve it. Job! Of course, he is a struggling writer who plays the guitar sometimes for a local band called Sea. He lives in a room in the house of an 80 year old widow, Samantha. She plays Dean Martin all day and he can smell old people walking in and out and sometimes, cats and dogs, too. He likes her. She lets him be but only till the end of the month. On the first day of every month, he finds her waiting by his door - the whole 4 feet 9 inches of her stooped body, supported by a walker, asking for the rent. It is nominal and he finds a way to pay every month. He does not like to disappoint her. After all, she is the only woman in his life. His Ma left him trying to teach him art. Ebbie left him for art. And now he is here.

I also know that he wears a bracelet on his right wrist. He got it when he was 16. It gets stuck in his hair but he wears it, anyway. It was from his first love. The one that never makes it to the last. That one.

It says *veni vidi amavi*. And he wears it even though it embarrasses the 32 year old man that he is.

Let alone his friends. He has two. Max and Portia. They meet on weekends at Starbucks on Callowhill Street. Smith has to walk a lot to reach that place but it has memories and he is a hoarder. The band on his wrist is a sign enough, I guess. In the last chapter, he left his bag in Starbucks.

He always turns the tap the wrong way before figuring out the right way, he hums tunes he makes up on his own while writing, he writes mostly in Fairmount Park or in the light of the table lamp of his room with a can of Yuengling beer. He is a beer person. He cannot have many one night stands because of Samantha and he does not have the patience for something serious since Ebbie. He is scared so he hates art. He changed his desktop cover from Bosch to a picture of Delaware. Water never deceives. It is transparent.

So, Smith ends his day in beer and begins it in words. He takes Samantha's dog for a walk sometimes. Timmy is a good furry kid who is always nestled at Samantha's feet.

He likes that smell- wet dog, old woman and beer.

Somewhere, Dean Martin sings and he writes/types in his room.

For now, that is all I know.

Let's see if I get more answers on our next walk.

2:08: A.M.

Like I said, Smith makes me forget. The Fiction Workshop. So, they want me to flesh out his character before them but Smith is mine. Does it make sense? He is all I have been holding on to for so long.

He is all I have control over. He is my balance. I cannot hand it over to that girl who always scoffs at my use of the pronoun 'he' for Smith. She said give him a name and I did.

Did not change how I felt about him at all.

They asked me to try and be different.

I tried that too.

I changed my music.

I stopped painting.

I started smoking.

I tried random hook ups.

I tried meditation.

I tried smoking up, again.

I read autobiographies of poets and authors and tried being like them.

So, I got Bukowski tattooed on my left breast- a bluebird. I have no idea what it is doing there when what I wanted was that cheesy *veni vidi amavi* I find on Smith's wrist.

I looked into the mirror and I saw a terrible fish for long because of Sylvia.

I took roads I did not like because of Frost. I don't think Frost has been to Mumbai. Stick to the streets you know here- advice to the wise.

And more because of Kerouac.

I looked into purposiveness without a purpose because of Kant but that did not work for that specky guy in my workshop.

I suspended belief because of Coleridge but that did not work for the mother of two at the workshop.

So, after trying for months, I am leaving.

Smith and I left them today because we need to breathe.

Someone told me to stop living through others. So, that is exactly what I am going to do.

And before I am corrected, Smith is not an 'other'.

He is mine.

For now, that is enough.

⁕

Dec 26, 2016

Dear Elixir,

Thank you for last night. I should have brought you a gift but Carol never told me it was your birthday. I am glad I came, anyway.

Sorry I left before you woke up. I will explain it later should you want me to.

Call me on 8222xxxxxx.

Take care,

Roger

PS- I don't know what you like to eat but I made some orange juice. It is in the fridge and should help with the hangover. Or not. Works for me, though.

⁂

#12
Dec 26, 2016
11:00 P.M.

I hate birthdays. They always remind me of people I have loved and lost. I think that is why I began writing. Not birthdays. But people who left or who I forced out of my life.

Mum left before I even learned of her absence. Pa left when I was too busy being present. And Tom I literally threw out of the door. So, I write because of that. Initially I wrote only about myself. I wrote what I thought I knew and that felt good. It was cathartic but it was always about me. Now, I was writing the story of another but he was becoming mine too.

I made him sit when I wanted to. He fell in and out of love when I liked. He changed his job when I asked him to think about it. I might have been having a conversation with him but basically, I am conversing in my mind. Is it time to see a doctor? Am I Schizophrenic yet, or Bipolar? Will that validate my literary genius? Can I Woolf my way through this? But I love her. Can you ever really be who you love?

If that is the case, then I cannot be Smith. I love him but he is slipping through my fingers or maybe I am not holding tight enough.

He is slipping because my hands are sweaty with the freshness of yesterday. I have a new face in front of me now. And Smith's flick is not hiding this face anymore. I can see him clearly.

His skin is the colour of coffee. Just the way I like it- it has two spoons of milk floating in water and coffee powder. He has a two day stubble covering the area below his lips, the lips he parts occasionally to display a stack of white teeth yellowing at the edges. He smokes, this one. His hair is pulled back and long enough to stay that way without any gel or mousse. At least I did not touch any last night and it stayed like that as long as I remember till I pulled at it. So, he is tall, at least 4 inches taller than I am. So that makes him 6 feet tall. It made kissing easy. It has been a while since I was with a man who matched my height comfortably. Nobody had to bend awkwardly in a drunken state to fit. It was easy. He wanted to be a writer but he knew better, so, now he teaches English in a school.

I don't know why he moved here but I know he has lived here longer than I have.

He also has strong arms but a paunch. When I asked, I think he said something like 'beer belly' and laughed in between kissing my neck. So, his stubble stung. Not tickled but stung and so did the sex.

It did not tickle, but it stung. I had not had any in a while and then Carol brings this guy to my birthday party and I end up doing him. What I did not realise was that, I was undoing myself. I liked the feel of a man on my body after so long. Did I mention, he smokes? A little too much, but that is not half bad. It has its own smell. He takes Dunhill because he likes spending on the finer things in life. I took a drag from his cigarette last night. I liked the smell he left on me. His half burnt cigarette is still there on my bedside table along with my bra. Now, I also know that he does not clean up after him.

The face is clear. The mind, hidden.

But the face isn't leaving mine. I want to know the mind, too. I guess there is only one way to find out.

Get that fucking faucet fixed and write.

*

Dec 26, 2015
My EB,

Your surprise awaits you at your favourite spot by Delaware at 10 P.M.
Bring your pretty little ass, there.

Love and all that jazz,
Tom

PS - Happy Birthday. You make waking up easier. Keep the smiles coming? Somebody might be living through them.

⁂

#13
Dec 26, 2016
2:32 P.M.

Roger left a note that I just found. Would I have been happier to see his frame yellowing in the sun on my white sheets? Obviously.

But the sheets still smell of his cigarette and Old Spice and a wet dog. Ginnie is on the floor so I am guessing that is him too. I like it, I think.

This is my writer's journal but I am born of all these things, so I think this cuts it. And my Professor wouldn't mind that this journal has some personal memories thrown in. Roger reminds me a little of Ned. I never wrote back to Ned because he still thinks of me as the vampire lover. But with Roger, I can start afresh. With Smith, I tried but he left me. He escaped. I think he left me for the hills. I came back, alone. And now, there is Roger. Everything can be new again. Everything.

So, I think I will call him in the evening. Maybe, he can come over and we can make some orange juice together and smell like wet dogs together and then smoke a cheap *beedi* in the balcony of my room. We will see where it goes from there.

Roger made me write better too. This morning words came easily. Let me meet him tonight and I will flesh out ideas, here, tomorrow. I am sure I will know more. At least now I don't have to talk to my mind. I can talk to a person. It has been a while.

⁂

CHAPTER 8

She changed my name, again. I am not Smith, now. I am Roger, a guy she met last night.

She brought him back to her dreams and I met him there.

But I do not mind the change to the rolling tongue for an *r*, the gaping hole of a mouth for *o* and the one lessening for the *g* and the *e* to find a way back to the rolling *r*. The name does not matter.

So, I do not know if Roger is the first name or the last.

But all I know is I was christened again.

She likes making me new.

Like that pile in the dustbin that I escaped to? I am renewed every time.

And so I change.

I move along pages as someone new.

Sometimes I move to the beginning, sometimes she

chooses to jump to the end.

But the end changes so I do not have to mention it, yet. I live in change.

I never thought she liked Smith. She always pressed the keyboard a little too hard when she wrote that name. It was always whispered with heaviness. Not the heavy breathing after sex, but the heavy breathing after running up the stairs when you realise you have forgotten the keys to your car. It was an exasperated heaviness - tired, weighed down. The kind that is gulped down by a Sula if the wallet does not comply. It was that.

I wonder if she ever thinks what I feel about this. What I feel about being changed just when I began to recognise myself. I move along the string holding together the frame of her book like a loose syllable slipping off an orgasmic tongue. I move along like that, too. Surrendering; vulnerable; ecstatic. I have nowhere to be. Nowhere to go till she takes me. So, I stream along the string and find a way in a new sentence benched under a new dog ear, blotched with ink pressed a little too hard, or a typo entered in a frenzy of inspiration. I live in those mistakes and corrections.

She controls me and that makes her happy. She smiles after making her edits. She presses the keys heavily even now, but this is with the eagerness of an embrace, one after running that extra mile for yourself, the one of celebration.

So, this new Roger, smokes a cigarette looking out the window of his blue apartment in a grey building, every night after work. A guilty escape, as the moon escapes the stars to shine behind a smoky cloud of his own mouth.

That is the only change.

Now, I smell like her.

I can live with that. For some time.

#14
Dec 27, 2016
11:40 A.M.

I used to talk to books. I spoke to Hank Chinaski and Arturo Bandini. I was almost convinced they knew each other. Of course, I didn't know then that Bukowski admired Fante.

With them the cocoon felt like a hammock.

I think they used their alter ego as hammocks, too.

Like it is easier to talk to a stranger, it is the easiest to talk through a stranger.

I don't know if it is a wise choice ethically or aesthetically, but it is a foolproof medium to be honest.

To bare your soul - to be messy, dirty, ecstatic, sexy, and political - all through someone else - someone you create - someone who speaks through you.

We already hide too much so why not extend that to an identity.

Hiding protects.

Hurt is directed towards the creation- the character is abhorred, not you.

But then, the character may be loved, too.

But don't we all want love? Don't we all want someone to tell us great things every day?

Have songs written on our eyes and hair; our principles; like John Mayer about the good girl who was crazy about Elvis?

But who will write a song on Bukowski? Or Fante?

Bukowski's bluebird might never meet the Beatles' blackbird in the same sky.

Maybe, because Bukowski's bird is caged or perched on his shoulder and the Beatles were busy teaching their blackbird to fly.

But what about Josephine Baker's Blackbird? The one outside her door, not flying and not caged? Singing the blues all day right outside my door.

I think Smith flew away with the Beatles. My bluebird is an impulsive tattoo on my shoulder.

I think Roger is like Baker's blackbird outside my door. The question is will I let him in?

⁂

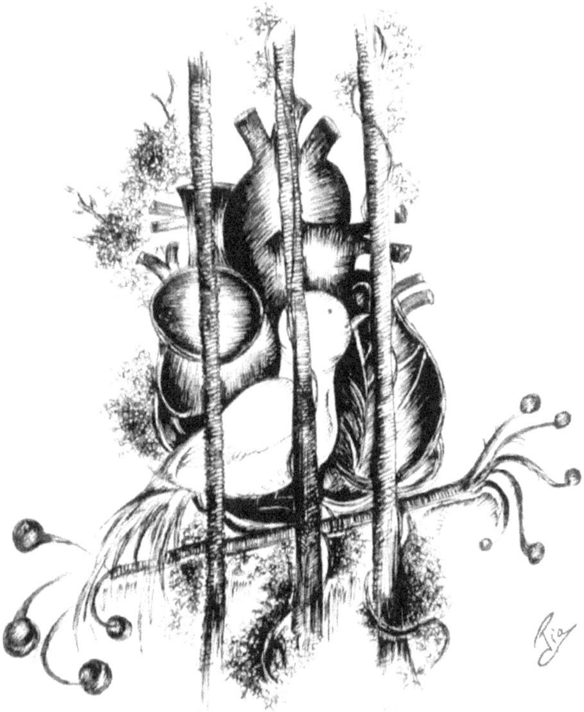

THE QUESTION IS WILL I LET HIM IN?

From: Ned Redford<Redford.Ned@writerscollab.in>
Date: Fri, Feb 17, 2016 at 12:09 AM
Subject: Important
To: elixir.banks3@gmail.com
Dear Elixir,

It has been a pleasure working with you over the last year. You are an incredible person with some great ideas in that head of yours. Keep them coming.

You know I am your Professor and therefore have to tell you certain things. You are behind your submissions and it is only because I care for you that I am letting you know rather than giving you an F right away.

Don't know what happened over the last two months. But I know for sure that the spark with which you waltzed into my office to discuss your ideas is missing and it worries me. I am an old man and have been stuck with writing long enough for nothing to trouble me, anymore. I have read terrible verse, promising prose, ridiculous plots, and refreshing characters - mind you, your ideas fall into all these categories - so much so, that nothing worries me anymore. Every year, someone will win the Booker, the Pulitzer, someone will have the most Facebook likes and Etsy sales and someone will write bestsellers. Publishers will print and readers will read. What worries me, is that you will stop writing.

Do not do that. Even if your ideas are like a bad hangover. Drain them out. Puke. Do not gulp them back in. It is from *that Kafkaesque bizarreness you hide, that your Bluebird will be freed.*

Do not lose your wonder. Anais Nin did not, so you are forbidden to, too.

Just please, write. Waltz and write. Sing and write. Drink and write. Walk and write. Eat and write, Shit and write. Sleep and write. Choose what you want, but, please just write.

I know you are going through a rough patch and that you are dropping out of the course. I know I might not be seeing you for very long, but the note you left on my desk makes me write this to you.

Elixir, be good to yourself, but first be good to the writer you want to be.

You are stifling her right now. Please, let her be stupid. Let her be reckless. Let her think that a paranormal romance can make sense. 'Bram Stoker, Tim Burton made it work,' you told me when I dismissed your idea at the beginning of the semester. Let her believe all those ridiculous things. It will help her breathe.

And maybe, while breathing and living, she writes a story that can actually impress me.

Imagine a world like that.

Write.

And write to me if you want to. I will be happy to rip your writing apart. It is one of my greatest pleasures.

Warmest wishes,

Ned

※

CHAPTER 9

I do not have a birthday.

There was a party for her birthday, yesterday.

(I like that I understand time now. Even though it does not make a difference to me, I like knowing when I wake up and when I am made to go back to sleep. Or when I am lying awake.)

She murmured into the pages how she dreaded these socially awkward gatherings, clothed in self-indulgence and maybe, loathing drowned in excessive drinking and the smell of hash. She liked the nakedness of solitude that we had. The pages, me on the pages, her hands on me, on the pages. We liked it like that.

But she played along. Laughed when someone said something funny. She danced when the music let her sway. She also kissed him when the wine had its way.

I do not have a birthday.

23 October. I thought that was my birthday. But I had a little death soon after, when she threw me in the bin.

25 November, I was born again.

December 2, I was made Smith.

26 December, I was born again as Roger.

I do not know the idea of being born as something that happens once and validates celebration.

I know of it as something that is born out of change, like when I was flung into the bin. Or when I was retrieved... Also, when I was christened again. And again. And maybe, again...

So, my birth was not in the tree that made the page or the desk that laboured me into existence. I think my birth is every day as we move along the umbilical cord of the string holding the pages of her journal together, or the fingers that carry her thoughts from her head to the screen. I am born every day.

But with every change, I die too. I die and am resurrected.

I wonder what it will be like when she ceases to write. Will that be my death? Will Roger live?

Let us not mull over that tonight.

I hope she makes Roger smoke into the moonless night, tonight.

I also hope she spills her Sula onto the screen, tonight.

Anything to numb the question.

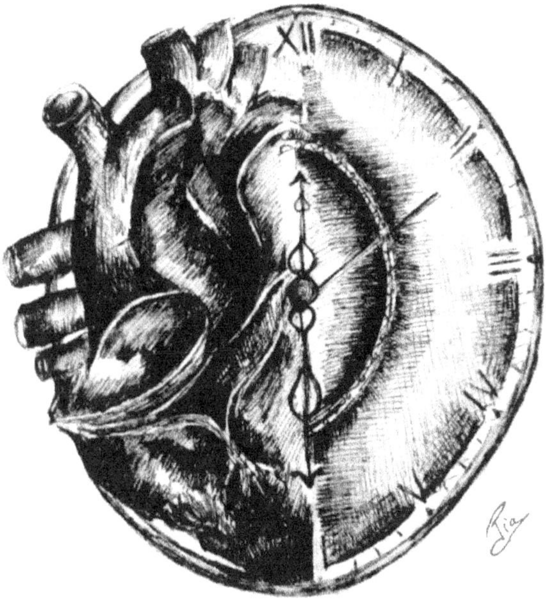

I LIKE THAT I UNDERSTAND TIME NOW.

#15

Jan 1, 2017

3:00 P.M.

The first poem I ever learnt was Daffodils.

I wandered lonely as a cloud...

Roger told me today about teaching this poem in his class of 11 year olds.

It was not in the syllabus but he isn't the kind of man who sticks to the curriculum. I know he will get into trouble for that but I guess he knows that, too.

And I can almost see him as a lonely cloud. It's easy.

He floats in the ash of his own cigarette smoke.

We have been spending all our days together. He comes over from school or I meet him where he is and we talk. Talk a lot.

I don't have time to be alone, anymore.

And that scares me. I used to be a lonely cloud too. I carried Smith like rain in my being to drench whatever thought I found worthy of wetness.

Now, there is another kind of wetness that only Roger quenches.

With him, I feel like I am on a hammock, again.

The cocoon all but forgotten.

But I do miss the sky being all about me.

I am waiting for him to get here and I don't like the impatience.

The comfort of being alone is that you never have to wait. But now, I spend my days waiting for his school to end and for him to get here so we can talk. Talk and have sex. Bum a smoke on the balcony and talk more. Just so I can talk to another human who doesn't like being peopled. It is refreshing to be with a person because of his hate for other people. It is like talking to a mirror, a mirror I wouldn't mind sleeping with every now and then.

I know Freddie always said that I take a free fall into a relationship - always too easy and soon. 6 days this time- a personal record.

But I don't know any other way. How can you not?

I could never walk downstairs into love. I always dived hoping to be caught. I know it is a ridiculous teenage clichéd thought, but I am not sure if there is any other kind... perhaps not in my books.

I know he won't be around for long. He is not the kind - but I like having him now.

Two lonely clouds meeting before we rain down on our respective lives - we make for a pretty metaphor and sometimes metaphors are enough.

I ALWAYS DIVED
HOPING TO
BE CAUGHT MID
FLIGHT

#16
Jan 2, 2017
2:00 A.M.

Roger took me to a gallery, today. I told him I am a little stuck and I don't know what to do with my novel. Did I mention that Roger used to write too? He took me to the gallery because he said it would help. How could I tell him that I have already tried artsy quirks in order to write and make sense? So, we went to NGMA this time. We gave Jehangir rest for the week.

We looked at a Souza for 22 minutes (yes, I timed it) because I could not understand this exercise and also because I had done all this. I had seen this and tried recreating it and cut open the canvas when I failed. This painting frustrates me. I want to go back to Bhaskaran's cats but Roger does not let me move. He has the answers so I stay with him.

Francofonia spoke about portraits and what they hide. I cannot see any of that. I only see Roger right now. I am new in his world and I like that, almost like this birthday I was reborn. He has a wife but they don't live together. Not in the same room. It has been 4 years. He also has a 6 year old son. I want to meet him but I cannot. Obviously. What will his wife think? So, I travel 2 hours every morning to see him in one of these two galleries in Kala Ghoda for my answers because at home the leaking faucet is waiting.

And I have not heard the *tak tak tak* to drown it in a while. I feel like I am drowning and I am hoping Roger will pull me out.

So, I know that Roger has a life apart from the one he shares with me. I am his escape. Was Smith, mine? Is Roger the new escape or the destination? Is he the road or the pothole?

I don't have answers to all those questions but I have other answers - Why his first novel failed and he left writing? Why his wife cannot stand him anymore? Why he doesn't like smoking but can't leave it? Why he never lets me meet him at a hotel and insists on coming home? Why he doesn't bathe every day? Why he listens to the same song on loop while making love? Why he never finishes his Kingfisher Premium and leaves the last sip parched in the bottle? What colour is his dream car? What about the sea draws him? Why is he in Mumbai? What does he call his son with love? What does he call his wife when she is not around? Why his students adore him? What is his favourite midnight snack? Why he is a staff room misfit? Why he likes having sex on the floor more than the bed? What the beach does to him? What taste he likes to lift off my lips? Why he smells like a wet dog? I have these answers but I am not sharing them with anyone because Roger feels like mine and only mine to keep. So, on the screen and on my bed, I keep him as mine. I cannot share him even with the pages of my diary.

And that is fine.

CHAPTER 10

We go to a gallery every now and then. She likes looking at portraits.

Faces fascinate her. Faces she has not known but can see. She saw a clip from Francofonia three times to hear what it had to say about portraits. Finally, someone agreed. Even if that was a screen different than the one she has been pouring her heart out to.

I look at these portraits too. The same artist. Different faces. All of them look at the viewer in the same way. But all of them say something different. I wonder if Roger said something different than Smith did to his reader. Where does my voice rest in all of those persistent echoes? Where does it escape to in the gaping holes of Roger's o and the curves along Smith's *m*? She is the artist. Am I her canvas? Or her paint? Or the brush? Or am I the painting? There is no Smith to answer these questions now. But I doubt the bag leaving imbecile would have been of help. Roger just rolls a gaping hole in paper and fills it with tobacco. That does not answer questions… but it silences them.

Maybe, that will do for now.

#17
Jan 5, 2017
2:31 A.M.

I made Roger hear Mom's song. He forced me to sing one of mine. I have nothing on Mum but I made him hear this soppy song I wrote when I first moved here about making a new home. It is not complete but he liked it. He said it is 'our song'. So 'mine' became 'ours'. I couldn't tell him that I wrote it hoping someone in Philly singing by the Delaware will come make it his, again. I don't know how I feel about it. I don't want to. I am going to write a little because I have more answers and no squeaky Ebbie or silent Samantha looking over my shoulder while I handle Smith's story. So, I am taking control of Roger on the screen. It is the story of movement and love and life and change from this man's perspective - like a 50 page monologue. A novella. Roger could not write his story and now I will write his. It will be my gift to the man with answers.

Clichéd, I know. But then, what isn't?

The song: *for those who want to read (ri:d/) it-*

Let's make a home...

Out of papers stashed in dreams...

Of a ceiling of my summer dress...

And floor of your jeans...

The tapestry is your choice...

The music will be mine...

Let's put up our pillars...

And engrave 'ever mine, ever thine'...

Get the lilies for my garden...

I will get us our bunk...

Get me semal for my hair...

I will get your old monk...

⁂

LET'S MAKE A HOME..
OUT OF PAPERS STASHED IN DREAMS.

CHAPTER 11

Where is she today? The screen has been opened from its slumber with the keyboard for two hours now. But she is not around. Did she go for her own slumber with her own Roger? What about the one she left on the screen looking at the estranged keyboards? What about me?

I hear her as the keys jingle against the door. She rushes in and begins typing. I think she missed me.

I think she missed thinking about me. Her hands run across the keyboard as I run across the pages.

She plays Dean Martin in the background today, giving Damien Rice a rest.

I wonder where Damien in that LP rests tonight as Dean comes to life.

He sings as though he has been woken up from

sleep and his lullaby is putting me to sleep as she writes about things around me.

I sleep on the screen under the ticklish movement of letters across my bodice.

I will sleep smiling, tonight.

I can live with that.

#18
Jan 7, 2017
1:06 A.M.

I have more answers, now. Roger is making my story for me and he doesn't even know that.

He is a little distant but that is because his son is sick and he is taking care. Apparently, his wife is an alcoholic (another flavour to the story) and he cannot leave his son. I said I will like to meet him but I am not allowed. That is okay because then I can drown the *tip tip tip* in the *tak tak tak* of typing and the story just drips from my fingers.

I trust the Roger I have come to know as well as the one I create. So, I know I am safe.

My prospective publisher, the plumber, Ginnie's doctor, Roger's son - no one unsettles me anymore...

Except Freddie. He does not approve of Roger. So, I sent him a list of things that make Roger good for my writing. I also sent him Prof Redford's mail to convince him that I must keep writing no matter how bizarre my ideas are. His last mail had hope. I think he will come around.

Because I am sure. I have suspended disbelief in Roger. He is real and good. A person who answers more than he asks. Now, that is a find. Also, he is great in bed. Not just at sex but the conversations that follow. He does not turn his back on me to sleep from exhaustion or cuddle forcibly. He just lies down on his side of the bed leaving the other side for me, lights a cigarette and lets me ask questions. He never asks. I think he knows I don't want to tell.

He knows me and now, I don't need a figment of my imagination or Freddie or letters or Tom's songs to do that. He does that for me.

I don't even have to drink because Roger is my new elixir. I don't need music because his words are all the melody I need. I don't need the leaking faucet because with him, I am banked.

*

Take Care.

CHAPTER 12

She always keeps a book of Coleridge's poetry on her bed side. Sometimes she carries it with her to the desk with the laptop like she carries me through the day in the folds of her mind.

Samuel Taylor Coleridge, The Complete Poems (Penguin Classics)

She loved the mariner. She believed that he could exist. Her eyes responded to his appearance in the poem with the same excitement that I meet her with every time she begins to type.

I believe in her too.

She changes me and erases a part of me. She brings me back from the bin and makes me new. But through it all, she always makes me. Like I am her mariner. A mariner with a cigarette dangling from his parched lips and a moonless night for company. I am her mariner.

And she is the ocean. She is my elixir. She is my Elixir and now, I am banked.

And I can live with that, for now.

Text received - Roger
11-1, 19:52

I will call you when things get better.

Take care.

CHAPTER 13

She doesn't hear me well anymore.

I am sure she tries but something is coming in the way of our conversations.

I think I am being too persistent. Maybe, she needs a break.

It has been us for far too long. But what am I to do when she is not around.

I swim across pages to know how we got here.

Things look acceptable to me. Yes, she changed my name a while back but she still dreams of me so I am there in her life. Somewhere in the shadows but still there.

I am learning words too while I wait.

Words with which I can answer some of her questions.

She has so many but I have more.

There is too much noise right now with us because

the two of us are talking at the same time. Always, asking - never listening - Maybe that is why she is away.

Maybe, that is why she is far.

Perhaps, I should quieten down so she comes back.

And we talk, again.

Back and forth.

From her to me.

#19
Jan 12, 2017
1:13 A.M.

Nowadays, writing feels like running on the treadmill with someone else setting my pace.

Alone was good. This is unsettling.

I am on a 4 on some mornings and then suddenly it is a 10 and I fall of.

Then, I lift myself up and jog to a 6 before I am made to crawl to a 2.

I am running without any control and I am falling in the absence of any.

I pant too with the exhaustion of passivity. More questions. No answers.

Always more; never less.

I am drowning in my sweat but I can't stop running.

The treadmill won't stop.

Or start.

I can't tell.

⁂

#20
Jan17, 2017
1:07 A.M.

I have not seen Roger in 10 days. He has not answered my calls. Not all of them, at least. He has left some texts unanswered but just some. Carol says he is busy with his son or daughter- I don't know and I don't care or maybe I am drunk and my Sula does not care. I need more answers and I am not getting any. What am I to do?

I miss him, too. Bitterly. Habit is a strange creature. It holds on to you like a cigarette dangling from your lips. It will fall only if you part your lips enough. Do I want to part my lips enough? Am I ready for that? Am I ready for Roger to go? Am I ready for the story to end without its teller? Am I ready to write without him? I don't even have my figment of imagination or Freddie or letters or Tom's songs. I said I didn't need them because he was here. But he is not and Ginnie is all I have curled up on my bed. I guess, she was left abandoned when the bed was occupied by Roger. Now, she has her side back but mine feels empty even when I am lying down on it.

The faucet is louder than the rain tonight and I need to get it fixed before it deafens me.

It is time to fix the faucet because I am not writing, again. And no Professor Redford can make it better. It is the faucet. Always was and always will be. So, I will call the plumber.

And get all this sorted. And I will call Roger too.

I need answers or I will let the cigarette fall from my lips.

I should listen to Freddie. I should listen to Tom's songs. I should read letters. I should look at Ginnie and know she feels abandoned. I should let the cigarette go.

2:22 A.M.

I dreamt of Smith. Where was he and where did I leave him? He was following me wherever I was going. He looked sad behind the flick that covered his right eye – he chose right, eventually. He followed me to the grocery store close to the road side restaurant where everyone drinks. He followed me to the Goregaon station. He came with me to the gym. He bought vegetables with me. He walked two steps behind me all the way to the Gobind Nagar turn towards my building. He followed me till the door of my house but he did not come inside. Because inside the cigarette stood reclining against the fridge sipping orange juice.

And I woke up after that. I think I should see a therapist. Or call Freddie. It is the same thing. For now, Ginnie is good and warm.

⁂

THE BAND ON HIS WRIST IS A SIGN ENOUGH, I GUESS.

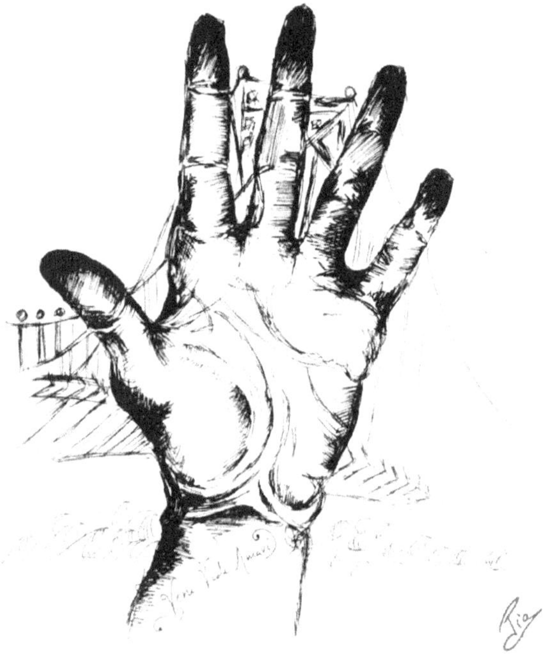

#21
Jan 18, 2017
Afternoon

I hate not knowing.

That is why I chose to be alone with Ginnie. With her, I always know what's going on.

Freddie couldn't keep secrets. Tom didn't want to keep any which is why we ended.

I created Smith because I wanted to know everything. I write because of that.

I haven't called Carol because I never know what's happening with her.

I don't know why Roger isn't calling to tell me what's happening with him. Like I said, I knew he wouldn't be around for long, so I am not surprised.

I cannot keep anyone, anyway. I have known that.

I just hate not knowing.

What am I to do with a story that is half complete?

What am I to do with unanswered questions?

Who will write my story for me?

I hate not knowing.

⁂

CHAPTER 14

There is disquiet. A lot of it. There are too many voices, now. There are too many characters, now.

I cannot hear her questions over their careless breathing. It is getting crowded and all of us are trying to breathe through congested lines. Trying to find our own story to be heard and made known.

We are specs of ink splayed on a paper benched onto a screen. But these crawling black ants on the screen are too many and too close together. The gaping holes meet each other at odd intersections and somewhere, I hear a gasp. Somewhere I hear someone collapse.

Somewhere I hear the words crash down like a pack of cards. I can hear pages strike against each other and crumble into separate shards.

I can hear a Roger. And a Smith. Somewhere a Lal Ji lingers and a Shanti too. I see lines stacked on top of each other like Philly, here too.

I see her too. She walks through a maze of things I do not remember. We were made new. What is all of this?

I cannot make sense of anything till the screen is separated from the keyboard and I wake up.

Did I dream tonight?
Did I dream like her?
I do not know if I can live with that.

#22
Jan 27, 2017
10:24 P.M.

The cigarette called. It is over. He didn't know it already was. His answers are still mine, so I am not sharing them. Not even with the diary, maybe, on the screen when I finish his story. I have only myself for the answers, now. And I am not half as bad. Before the cig, I had written 100 pages of Smith's story. It felt like mine. So, I am sure it was.

Also, yesterday, I got the faucet fixed. The plumber came over and the job was done in 15 minutes. So no *tip tip tip*, anymore.

All I have is *tak tak tak.*

So, I will return to Smith. Or the Smith I call Roger, now. The story seems okay. So I won't change it. I don't have time, anyway. Smith will understand. I will make him understand and we will be okay.

12:23 A.M.

I know why he left, but he left a gaping hole in my palm. We were not cheesy heart talkers. We weren't around for long to make it to the heart. For us it was the palm… with which he pressed my breasts and silenced my moans... The palm he traced with his fingers for answers he never asked me to give. The palm he let me rest my head on. The palm he wrote a song on but never shared with anyone. I won't share it either.

It escaped into the hole of my palm.

I don't know how the story ends.

I have no idea.

For answers, I have a running faucet, now. The plumber fixed it so it doesn't leak anymore but I can't spend my days without my soundtrack. So, I let it run.I did not know that without the sound of water, I will be crippled. So, I let it run. It is nice and warm like Ginnie.

And maybe that will do.

CHAPTER 15

13 days have gone by since she last wrote. I have been a rusting folder on a screen for 13 days. There must be someone else, but Roger is not in her world. There is no space for me but the tiny segment on a screen that is too close to the Recycle Bin that I am always scared of when the mouse runs over the surface of the desktop. The wine still sits on the table and I am scared it will throw me in the bin, again. After all, I have not been used in all of 13 days.

I have been erased not from the folder but from her dreams. So, she does not write anymore.

There are no dreams, anymore.

They sit benched at her pillow when she wakes up. They are all stacked one on top of the other while she stretches and extends her arms out like the rays of the sun.

The dreams melt in the sun and I wait.

It is not easy to be erased. It is harder still, to be ignored. I do not know what I am but I am there.

Right after being created, I am left at the edge of a screen.

Now, I know me. I think I do.

I was left open in the gaping holes of my letters and now these holes are what I scream through, silently and quietly. She cannot hear me. Can you?

#23
Jan 28, 2017
Late night

Memory moves.

It walks, sits, shits, cries, fucks, loves and gallops.

Memory moves from yesterday into today and sleeps its way to tomorrow.

And that is why nothing ends.

There is no clean break.

No closure.

Because memory sticks like a flying mosquito caught in the pages of a closing book. It sticks and becomes one with the paper.

It sticks and becomes one with you.

You move, it moves along. Like that dead mosquito.

So, none of them really left. They all still linger.

All of them with their marks on my palm, between my breasts, on my shins, on my head and my back. They are all still here and I am looking at disappointment if I am hoping for release.

Maybe, memory is more than nostalgia, a tool to remind us of all the things we did right and all the things we spoiled so we know how we got here. So, we live in a flux of torment and jubilation knowing that we have made the life we are living.

Some days we can smile along with all the marks.

And some days we can drown them with some wine.

It was one of those marks that told me, *in vino veritas.*

And I told him, *in aqua sanitas.*

But why must I always choose between health and truth? They can coexist, no?

Memory moves and we move along- like an oscillating pendulum, in a game of laughter and tears and whether you know it yet or not - it is all your doing.

So, I choose to pat my shin, head, back, palm and the space between my breasts when I am happy with what memory chooses to show me on a sunnier morning.

And I choose to cover all those bare parts of my past when memory reminds me of days I regret.

Let's see what tomorrow brings of yesterday.

⁕

#24

January 28, 2017

Even later

I can never keep anyone. Anyone.

It is just a pattern in life that has gone on for a little too long and I don't think I can change it.

The funny part is I don't think I want to change it.

I am okay in this pool of self-pity I have created. I am not drowning, so all the lifeboats coming my way are superfluous. I am okay, floating.

I should be.

It is like language - this peaceful abyss.

Things are close together. They are put close together to make sense when there isn't any to find.

A cat is called a cat because it is. Does it sound logical? To anyone? Does it?

But I guess, Q.E.D.

Names are like nude make up

-Unnecessary ornamentation.

Naming a character was the hardest thing I have done. I spent days deciding Smith should be called Smith. For a long time, he was Tyler but that was too 'high school' for him. Then, there was the time, I thought he should be called Cory but then I couldn't stop thinking about the unhappy Richard Cory.

Hank would have been too obvious for a fan girl and too embarrassing in front of people who know me. Holden will always be Salinger's. So, after exasperated attempts at novelty, I came up with the most commonplace name I know-lifted off the steward of my flight to Delhi - Smith.

I understood the importance of a name when I learned that Bombay was Mumbai and Chennai, Madras. Who am I kidding? I didn't understand even then.

All I know is that my passport allows a certain Elixir Banks to be in India for a while and this Miss Banks is in fact me.

Who decided that a big ball of fur meowing and attacking unexpectedly will suddenly be categorised as a CAT- a weird sound that begins with a lisp and ends with a bite.

If that wasn't enough, we moved from categories to specifics.

We are so obsessed with specifics - as writers, readers, humans.

Details. We love those little specifications that leave nothing to the imagination -

So I am Elixir. Before I even uttered a coherent word, I was made a life giving force.

An identity was forced onto me and for the rest of

my life I was supposed to live up to it.

"Live up to your name".

I can still hear Aunt say that.

I don't know how I wound up with her but then again, I had no say.

Much like everyone else - I had no say in who I ended up with and that is why I am happy alone.

Not happy, but happily sad in a blissful state of paradoxical self- pity.

What is the point of relationships when in the end nobody knows anyone? We are living together out of an acute fear of loneliness but is that enough to swim to the shore?

Carol says get to the shore - somebody is waiting. I did get to the shore but after the good old sex on the beach, everyone left - evacuated by a rescue helicopter... but I stayed - to swim back to pool - it is nice and warm. It feels real - I don't think I need anyone as long as there is the moon.

I am almost sure that the moon must feel warm, too.

After all it is shadowed by the sun.

There has to be enough fire in it to warm the tides.

And warmth is good.

*

#25

Jan 29, 2017

Around noon

Shanti Didi tries hard to talk in a language I understand.

Little does she know in not knowing she understands me more.

She never says, leave. She *says, liebe.*

Like she never says Elixir, but Elijir.

Like she never says house, but hose.

She never says leave but *liebe.*

And I love it.

I love her disregard of the arbitrariness of language that she leaves or *liebe-s* in her awkwardly fractured diction. Its musical or *musixal.*

So, I don't have to leave the door open. I have to *liebe* the door open.

I have to love the door open.

I have to pry it open with my intruding hands and *liebe* it.

Hold it. Rest my head against it.

Rest my heaving bosom against it.

I have learned to *liebe* the door.

It is the same door that someone you might *liebe,*

leaves from.

It is the same door that someone leaves from when you learn to *liebe*, again.

Roger walked out the same door a while back.

I don't think I knew him long enough to love him.

But I didn't want him to leave.

You see, this is what happens when you walk to the shore from the pool made by warm tides.

You are left marooned.

It is not him I miss. I think. I am almost sure...

I miss myself when I was with him. I miss myself when I was with Tom. Or Pa.

Or Redford. Or Freddie.

I miss Elixir the way they know her. And it is frightening to miss yourself.

If I am missing myself then who am I at present?

Do I become an 'other' just because I have another idea of self?

How do you live with an 'other' inside your palm?

But I miss her. Roger took her with him and now I am clutching onto the door for her to come back.

For her to regret leaving.

To regret loving.

I wish I could paint a trompe l'oeil door for myself

to walk in and out of. Leaving would be one sided then.

Alone, I am safe.

Together, I am lost.

Makes sense?

Maybe.

CHAPTER 16

Being written is like swimming- a tireless lap through pages and the minds of the writer; through leaking finger tips and drenching screens. If you stay underwater too long, you can run out of breath. That is what it feels like when she is not writing. There are days when she doesn't. Days at length and I am left gasping in the blues of her silence.

But then she wakes up and writes with the ferocity of a starved nymphomaniac and I am left panting.

She pauses and I float for a bit.

That helps.

I like floating.

It helps me prepare for a long dip or for hurried laps- whatever she prefers.

Being written, more than swimming, is like being in water.

Suspended.

I used to like that before.
But I sense that the lap is ending.
And I am not so sure anymore.

SHE PAUSES AND I FLOAT FOR A BIT.

#26
Jan 29, 2017
12:33 A.M.

The faucet is fixed. Roger is not here.

Ginnie has pee-d on the floor. Roger is not here.

Shanti Didi has cleared the table for breakfast. Roger is not here.

My cigarettes are over. Roger is not here.

I am going to take a shower. Roger is not here.

I am going to finish the manuscript, today. Roger is not here.

I am going to write to Freddie. Roger is not here.

I am meeting Carol later in the day. Roger is not here.

My Sula is finishing and Carol will complain. Roger is not here.

It rains almost every night. Roger is not here.

I cannot find my one size fits all bra. Roger is not here.

The bed is messy. Must clean it. Roger is not here.

I need to pick groceries because the fridge is an apology. Roger is not here.

I finished reading my second set of Betty and Veronica. Roger is not here.

I didn't know that Weatherbee wore a wig. Roger is not here.

And Jughead is a celibate. Roger is not here.

Okay, I made that one up but still, Roger is not

here.

Lumineer's Ophelia is playing on loop. Roger is not here.

Ben Zaidi is good for my ears too. Roger is not here.

I cannot find the Dean Martin record. Roger is not here.

Cliff Richard is still there between Bob Dylan and ABBA.

So, Smith... I lost him, too. Roger is not here.

I dream of him, sometimes. That is confusing.

By him, I mean Roger and Smith.

So, it should be them.

But they are the same.

Because both of them are not here.

I am alone. At last.

That should be enough. That is what Pa said. That is what Tom asked me to be. That is what Freddie wants back.

That should be enough.

⁂

ROGER IS NOT HERE.

CHAPTER 17

There is passivity. Time drags.

And I had just started understanding time. I wish I didn't.

Not much has happened in my already static life and I am worried. Is she done writing me?

Is this the end? I thought I would know when I am complete. How can you not?

But I know nothing. Again.

I am back to knowing nothing- a full circle.

If this is what complete feels like, I want to go back to not knowing.

I liked not knowing.

There is a promise of continuity in doubt as against the finality of knowledge.

I want to be ignorant, again. I want to leave my bag or Smith's bag in places again. The hills were a nice place to go to. I want to see them, again. I want to know

Roger, again. I want to be thrown into a dustbin again so I know the story is unfinished and I will come back.

Where do I go now if I am not coming back?

Am I coming back?

Is there a place to come back to?

Questions without answers. Only this time, all the questions are mine.

#27

Jan 30, 2017

Sunset

I was told in that Fiction Workshop I went to that I am too self-indulgent.

I spend my days writing in front of a laptop the thoughts I dream of in my sleep.

Of course, I am.

But then, what about Smith.

If I am the one, then is he the second?

Is he the other, because I am the self?

I don't know what the world means by be one with your character.

If that was the case then every written piece would have been a memoir or an autobiography

Then what is fiction?

There was a time I was vain enough to sit in my room, write and think that all thoughts escaping my pen were original.

In a world of 7.6 billion people and counting, how can I assume that nobody thought what I thought of today. What is this obsession with originality?

What is the point in the pursuit of knowing that it

is an aimless excursion?

So, I choose the mundane occurrence of a day to talk about and that, THAT makes me self-indulgent not the vanity in claiming originality.

When you avoid humans and spend days talking to a leaking faucet, a diary, a fictitious character and your pet bitch, I think you forget what human interaction feels like. I forgot what humans think like.

Then why am I writing all this.

What is the point?

Who is going to read it?

Not the straying water in my sink, or the ink etchings in my diary or Ginnie.

Some humans sitting far away will call me self-indulgent and the whole story will begin, again.

Stories. Now those, they love.

PART 2

THANATOS-

Begin again? So, die first.
To know water, learn of thirst.

From: Kaveri Tandon <k.tandon@kaveripublication.in>
Date: Fri, Feb 27, 2017 at 12:09 P.M.
Subject: Re: Manuscript - If Cities Were Mirrors
To: elixir.banks3@gmail.com

Dear Miss Banks,

I am happy to inform you that your manuscript has piqued our interest, yet again because of its raw intensity and simplicity. Kindly review the Letter of Intent attached herewith. Please let us know when you will be able to discuss the future of your work with our team.

Looking forward to hearing from you.

Regards,
Kaveri

⁂

IF CITIES WERE MIRRORS...

Dear Smith/ Roger/ he or whoever you were,

This is going to be long so bear with me. I have a lot to say. You probably know, already.

For what it's worth-I realised I never wrote to you. I wrote about you but I never wrote to you. I asked you questions and you never answered. This letter will be like this, too. You will not write back with unknown answers you took away with you when you escaped to hide in the crevices of the pines splayed on the floor on our way to McLeod Ganj. That is the first time I thought I had lost you. The very first time.

I had carried you like I carry my shin with me wherever I go. I say the shin because I am not always aware of its presence in me but it is always there holding me up and straight, making me walk, run. The calves hurt but the shin just supports. You were that to me before you left me for the hills. But I think I left you, too. I didn't try hard enough to keep you... I didn't echo you back to me. I didn't let you whisper what you wanted into my ears. Did you want to stay longer? You could have just asked. Maybe, I would have stayed. I would have stayed and you would have never become Roger and we would have finished another story... together.

I don't know if the publisher would have liked it. I am not sure if the readers would have bought it. But I would have kept you as mine.

Smith, you were my first in many ways. I remember thinking about writing my first novel when I was 6 and maybe that is when your seed was planted in my head or a mole was planted on my shin close to the knee. You are that permanent mark. I can burn you and you will be gone from my skin. But I cannot deal with any more goodbyes. So selfishly, I am keeping this part of you. When did you grow up, Smith? When did you become the guy who was there for my lonely nights? You never gave up, now, did you? I threw you in a bin, I ignored you for days, I dropped ash on the screen and I even drowned you in Sula. I took you for walks to places where I wanted to go and made you wear clothes I wanted you to wear. You suffered a heart break because my story needed it and then you gave some because I needed it. You walked on stilts on the edge of my mind and I let you fall onto my shoulder, crawl into my blouse, slide down my cleavage and land on my stomach. I made you fall many times, Smith, but you always found a way back to the same rope at the edge of my mind, your stilts waiting for you. It is like you never wanted anything more. Pa wanted love that I was stupid enough not to give. Tom wanted loyalty that I threw away. Freddie wants my presence. Redford wants words from me. You just wanted me. Or so it felt.

I kept you as mine for long - under different names, headers and footers, chapter numbers, page numbers, titles, random journal entries. But now an e-mail from

Kaveri tells me that you are going to be shared. They have read you - the first ones to have read you. They want to discuss your future with me. What will happen to you? Will you live in hardbound or a paperback?

Will you miss the screen, Smith?

Will you live in another screen as a kindle edition? How much will I get for parting with you? How much will I take for copyrights over you? At least on paper you will still be mine. That should be enough, no?

But it is not. Because, like Ginnie, like that leaking faucet, like my shin, you have been there through more than I can remember. You might have seen my dreams, too. Do you remember them? Do you remember why I woke up in a sweat many a night? Do you remember why I did not sleep?

Smith, I made you out of words and I gave you words to say... but today I am going to give you my words. Just for you to keep, only if you could actually read this. I wrote this for my perfect love and I know we are not perfect, romantic or any of the things I had thought of, when I wrote it in the library, on Locust St., as a 19 year old, on a paper I tore off the back of Salinger's Rye. But you are the closest I have come to perfection and Pa tells me that Ma always said, 'No one is perfect till you love them.' Now, I don't know if I love you, or what love means. But let's just say that in the entire world that I saw, you were the only one always looking back at me. Always. So, unlike the love of music, or palms, ours was a love of stares much more powerful than those portraits at Jehangir Art Gallery. We looked beyond the eyes.

And that is what made it enough.

I wonder now what it would have been like to escape with you on the pages on the screen - to stay there suspended in belief with you. We could swim together. I could have had a new name. I could have disregarded time. I could have made your 'always' into our 'forever'. I realise I am writing like that 19 year old in The Library Company, again. But I liked her and I think you would have too. Or maybe you already knew her – you, the mole on the shin close to my knee. Did you stick around for her? Do you still see her? I want to hold her behind my eyelids and let her drain over my cheeks, once, so my cheeks can soak her back in. Maybe, then I will become her, again. Maybe, then, I will be 19 and we will still have 10 years to be with each other. Just each other. Now, that would have been enough. Maybe.

To us-
Page 3 to Page 93

I want to read to you and I want you to read to me.
Words that were written by others, but somehow made sense to the persons we became together.
You and Me. 'Us' as grammar would call this union.
Sex-as biology would recognize this communion.
Words-these are just words. Not the ones that are preserved for you and me.
Those are special.
Those are ours in a way that even the writer wouldn't know.
Those are ours in a way that even the writer can never own.
Own them.
Own us.
We are syllables of an iambic pentameter, dissipated by unnecessary lows only to pronounce ourselves.
We are vowels without which the consonants can never make language
You may be an 'a' and I a 'u'
but the distance of 3 alphabets doesn't matter.
We are more than distance, we are more than words...
We are the meaning the writer never meant. We are the writer who doesn't know her own self.
We are the pages of a book that she lost but eventually found.

Our little escape isn't for long, but that is enough.
So even if, you are page 3 and I am 93, we broke away from the bound of the book and found our little eternity.
So what if they glued us back to the bound?
The glue touches you and a stream of it breaks away to find me.
It touches me and I know I have been touched…
By you.
So I will read to know what happens to him when he walks into the hall, and you tell me what the writer has to say in her acknowledgement.
I know the world skips what you say, most often. But yours are the only words that matter...
To me.
Say your thanks, and I will narrate another's story;
Somewhere between hard cover and straying glue,
Between biographies and gratitude;
Between dog eared pages and bookmarks;
There is a running string that brings me to you…
-Banks

Dear EB, or should I say Elixir?

You dream in too many ways for me to know what you like but I always liked to think of you as Banks. Your last name. It told me that you belonged to something and I craved that. You belonged, somewhere. Maybe, in Tom's songs? Your father's bicycle? Your mother's song? By Delaware? In Roger's rolling paper? In Ginnie's blind eyes? You belonged, Banks.

But I never did. I always existed in between pages and your moods. I lay suspended on the screen waiting for you to conjure up some magic. I did not mind it at all. I trusted you. But you were all I knew. How could I not trust the only thing I knew? I heard what you made me hear. I saw what you wanted me to see. I went where you took me. I became red because of your wine and now that red runs through me. You made me, Banks. So, does that mean I belong to you?

Are you my home? Then why do I stay on a screen? Why am I being taken away from you? Am I your child, the trouble maker, who you are sending away to a boarding, bound in paperback? Am I you lover, like Tom, that you are choosing to discard over another story? Am I your friend, like Carol, who you do not care much about, but keep around till it suits you? Or am I like Roger, a painful memory that is too attractive to discard, but too dangerous to keep? I do not want to be Roger, Banks, because I do not want to leave. You see, the thing is I do not know how to do that. Every time you decided I needed to go, I found a way to come back. Whether it was your basketball throw to the bin, or the echo you left me with in the hills... I do not know how to leave. But I know you will make me and I will. You see, I don't know any other way to live. Live - If that is what I do. Maybe, I just exist. Maybe life is ending today and existence is beginning. Or maybe existence is ending today and life is beginning because now, I am complete. But Banks, I have never lived/ existed without you. Who will hold me in their dreams, now? Whose pages will I swim on, now?

You should never have made me Roger. Maybe then, we would never have been separated. It is not that I am in love with you. You do not even notice me. I am like a mosquito in Mumbai summers - a ubiquitous presence. But I do not know anyone else and from what I have learnt by living in your head, familiarity is better. It is recognisable and for me, that is difficult to achieve in the first place. I do not know if I will miss anything but maybe I will miss looking for home, for that sense of belonging, in you. I always thought of you as mine. But you are letting me go now. Maybe, you never were mine. I know now I will be a nomad, running through stacks and screens, each a new experience, each a new touch, each a new drink to taste and each, a distinct burn to feel from a new brand of cigarette, each a different colour of hair to fall asleep in, each a different playlist to listen to...

Did you know how scary it was when you did not return to the screen? I lived/existed in fear, Banks, a fear you would not know, because you were always with someone. When your Pa left, you had Ginnie. When Ginnie became a habit, you had Tom. When Tom left, you found the same home in Ginnie again. Then you had Carol and then you had Roger.

I only had you because the others on the screen were part of a story I did not know- a story you were making. So, I waited for my turn, to turn up on pages and I did every time you called me.

I do not know if I want to say goodbye, or hold on to you by your knee, or just fix myself in the space between your olive bed frame and white pillow. Or should I believe in you once again and let you let me go? Do you want me to travel, Banks? Like your mariner? Do you want me to get away from you, so I can be on my own? Are you like a mother letting her kid fly from the nest? Or are you like a lover, who knows this love is now toxic? Or are you like a friend who knows, that some time apart, will do us good? Or are you like Ginnie for me, blissfully aware of my presence, even when your eyes do not acknowledge it? Will your mind erase me like the screen erased me, or will you think of your winged child, bitter lover, understanding friend, renegade alter ego?

I do not know if I want to ask you for something as a parting gift. I think I already have my parting gift with me. Maybe it is my nomadic freedom, like Tom did... You always admired that about him. Maybe, you will grow to admire me too. That should be enough to last my travels. Will you be waiting at whatever form my ship docks at? I doubt. You would have moved on and maybe, I will be Smith forever. Maybe, I will not change. Am I scared of stagnation? I do not know. I only know what it is like to become. What happens after, I am yet to feel. I wish I could tell you once I have the answers.

Will I have answers now, or will I look for them through someone else, again? Banks, I am suspended again… but this time I am disbelieving.

I really do not know if there is anything I want from you, as you hand me over to someone else. But I think there is one thing that can keep a string running from me to you. Will you think of me, whenever you choose to give my space in your dreams, screen and life to someone new? Think of me even if it is for the slightest second? I would know I did not stick around for nothing, even though I had no other option. You see, validation might help, because I am going out into the world without your Sula for the first time and I doubt it will be easy.

Was it easy for you when you left Philly?

Banks, I do not know if you will be fine. I do not know if I will be fine. But I hope whatever we are, we are that together, so at least we are feeling the same things at the same time. I learnt to feel because of you and I would rather follow you there, if not otherwise.

- Smith

#29
Feb 28, 2017
11:58 A.M.

What do I do with a writer's journal when the writing is done? What do I do with myself when I am done writing? It is like today. 28th of Feb. A weird day.

Yesterday, I was counting the days till Lal Ji comes for the rent and I counted three. But it is Feb and I have no time. Just like that, my days were taken from me. Just like that, Smith was taken from me. Roger was taken from me. Ginnie will be taken soon. And that is also how my manuscript was taken away from me. My screen had the MS DOC that has seen more than I remember and I also have that crappy cover of my book to think of. MY book. But I don't HAVE it, anymore. Does it make sense? I don't have it because, now it doesn't need me. My work is done and the folder on my screen just looked at me, passively. So, I deleted it - put it in the recycle bin that was conveniently placed closed to it. One move to the right and it ended. Smith was dumped with Roger in a pile of garbage that I haven't had the time or patience to revisit. I cannot help my dreams. They appear sometimes but then it rains at night, sometimes, and they are drained away. Or, I don't sleep at all.

And I am reading Edgar Allan Poe, again.

"All that we see or seem is but a dream within a dream."

I just wish I could stand in front of his house to believe that. Maybe, it is time to go back. Maybe, it is time for Delaware again.

For how long can I drown sandal after sandal in the Arabian Sea? For how long can I imagine drowning myself in its waves, as they engulf my sandal and I let it go? Will it be that easy to let myself go too? For how long can I remain without my favourite lipstick? For how long can I wear a one size fits all bra? I want my bra, my fit, the one that lady on 6th street promised? For how long can I live through Shanti Didi, Lal Ji, the chemist, the shopkeeper hiding everything you can name in two racks, Ginnie and my screen? How long can I talk only to a diary?

So, what is the purpose of this diary? What is the purpose of living in Mumbai? What is the purpose of living at all - This strange illusion of home I carry in my heart. Should I drown that in the Sea too, or should I take it with me to Philly to drown it in Delaware?

Freddie might come along. He likes to humour me.

But what do I do with you, diary? I never gave you a name. As a kid, all my diaries had names. You were just a writing journal. I think I will call you Ginnie, the Second. Like her, you never left. Or Smith. But Smith, I sent away.

Do you want to come with me? I realise that you are not Smith or Roger and you don't answer, you only listen. So, I have to control the situation, here…

I think you can come. It might just be nice.

Or maybe I leave you here with my sandals in the sea.

Maybe, someday, someone will read you and you will validate my eccentricities enough to make me a writer. Redford would cringe at my gross generalisation, but then, he is not who I am and I cannot dream to be him. Dreams, Edgar Allan Poe, 7th street, Cliff Richard. fridge magnets; Rocky; white doors; Delaware; a school on Spring Garden St.

I don't know. I have to go somewhere.

To the sea?

To Philly?

I think you should come along.

Think about it. We could start something new. Maybe, I will make you talk too.

That will be nice.

What do you think?

-EB

⁂

...I WAS COMPLETE IN MY OWN BEING AND THAT IS WHAT SCARED THE WORLD...

Read.
(/red/)

So, I am Smith that was made into Roger. But now I am becoming someone else - because of you.

Who are you? All I know is that your skin is papery white and I am no different, as I stay benched between a hard bind. I have a string running through me holding the pages together. The string sometimes touches the shell I am left with, with a little red leaking from the centre. But that could just be the Sula that has been smeared over me over the last couple of years. It was from her.

But do you have something like that holding you together?

You touched the pages, sniffed the edges, dog eared my wardrobe and stripped me naked whenever you turned the page. You also drenched me in your tears and your soup when you read me in bed.

You made me an apparition in your dreams and sometimes I walk with you.

Am I becoming, again? Am I being made new, yet again? Is this another christening? So be it.

Sometimes, you sleep on me. Lose strands of your hair intersect with my words and I can smell Cherry Blossom, the one that Neruda romanticised? She had told me. Sometimes, I become the lose strands when I escape the pages and enter your dreams. But that is rare, because you have other preoccupations. I am your recreation. So, I have become a celebration. You do not discard me. You keep me as a prized possession on the table next to the sofa in your porch. There is only a photo of what looks like your family there, so I know it is an important place. Sometimes, you take me with you to the bathtub. I have never felt wetness before. Not by water, anyway. It was always wine or beer or soup or a dog's lick. But this wetness is different. It is like the tip tip tip of the faucet that she loved. It is water. At least it feels like that. Sometimes, you carry me around in a bag with a packet of half eaten chocolate biscuits, your comb with a few strands entangled between its teeth, a diary that you never write in, lose pens and your wallet, face wipes and a lipstick. Sometimes, you lend me to a friend. That is another story altogether. But you know displacement, because you have read the story I represent, three times already. Why? You do not answer my questions. They never reach you.

You like to take me to a busy market that leads to a fort sometimes. It is a strange place because the fort has etchings, not by craftsmen but by lovers. It overlooks a lake and the sun is always a little too strong for you. So, you wear your shades. What do I do with the glow when you spread me open under the sky and devour me word by word? The sun devours me too, her white, a little tan now.

The pages, yellowing a little with my tan. But you

touch me and no one before you did. So, it is new. It is a caress of papery over paper and in the space of a letter, I hang suspended in disbelief, again...

Hanging. Floating. Waiting.

Where else can I go?

A CARESS OF PAPERY OVER PAPER...